CROWN OF LIFE

CROWN OF LIFE

The Story of Mary Roberts Rinehart

By Sybil Downing & Jane Valentine Barker

ROBERTS RINEHART PUBLISHERS

Copyright © 1992 by Sybil S. Downing and Jane Valentine Barker
Published in the United States of America by
Roberts Rinehart Publishers, Post Office Box 666, Niwot, Colorado 80544

Published in the United Kingdom and Europe by
Roberts Rinehart Publishers, 3 Bayview Terrace,
Schull, West Cork, Republic of Ireland

Published in Canada by Key Porter Books
70 The Esplanade, Toronto, Ontario M5E 1R2

International Standard Book Numbers 1-879373-13-0 (cloth)
1-879373-18-1 (paper)
Library of Congress Card Catalog Number 91-66682

CONTENTS

Contents

ILLUSTRATIONS

Page 3: "For the first time in her life, her brown hair was out of braids and pinned on top of her head. . . . She desperately wanted to look grown up, for it was essential to make the right impression." Drawing by Ann W. Douden

Page 27: Pittsburgh and Allegheny Cities, from a map of 1890. Courtesy of the Historical Society of Western Pennsylvania

Page 57: "This house was like a prison. Her entire world consisted of its three floors, a demanding husband and three boys, a hired girl who needed supervision, and a noisy dog . . . and always Stan's patients." Drawing by Ann W. Douden

Page 89: Mary's map of the Front, dated February 23, 1915. Courtesy of the University of Pittsburgh Libraries, Special Collection Department

Page 103: "Riding with the general, she'd seen the men coming back from the trenches. . . . some bandaged, the white gauze strangely iridescent in the moonlight." Drawing by Ann W. Douden

ACKNOWLEDGMENTS

We owe our heartfelt thanks to a great many individuals, not the least of whom are George H. D. Rinehart and Frederick R. Rinehart for their personal insights regarding their distinguished grandmother and great-grandmother, respectively. We are grateful, too, for the enthusiasm and help of Dr. Warren Gillette, Dr. Donald L. Kellum, Doris Wolff, and Donald deKieffer who lent their particular expertise to the project.

We convey special appreciation to Mr. Charles E. Aston, Jr., head of the Special Collections Department of the University of Pittsburgh libraries for his invaluable assistance and support. Thanks also to Joseph F. Smith, archives chairman of the Sewickley Valley Historical Society and to the reference department of the Sewickley, Pennsylvania Public Library.

In addition, we wish to thank James S. Rush, Jr., Civil Reference Branch, National Archives, Washington, D.C.; Earl Old Person, Chairman, Blackfeet Tribal Council, Browning, Montana; David Walter, Director, Montana Historical Society; Clyde Lockwood, Director, Glacier Natural History Association; Tom White, Kay Gutman and Dr. W. Thomas White, curator, librarians of the Hill Reference Library of St. Paul, Minnesota; the reference department of the Historical Society of Western Pennsylvania, Pittsburgh, Pennsylvania; Trevor Link, librarian, Native American Rights Fund, Boulder, Colorado; Emily C. Walhout, librarian, Houghton Library, Harvard University, Cambridge, Massachusetts.

Be thou faithful unto death,
and I will give thee a crown of life.
Revelation 2:10

PREFACE

Crown of Life is a work of fiction. It is based on facts gleaned from Mary Roberts Rinehart's autobiography and other of her non-fiction books and articles, her correspondence and diaries, and her biography, *Improbable Fiction,* by Jan Cohn.

Mary Roberts Rinehart was born on August 12, 1876, only eleven years after the end of the Civil War, in the western Pennsylvanian town of Allegheny, across the river from Pittsburgh. That year the nation was celebrating its centennial. Custer and his men made their last stand on the windswept plains of the Montana Territory. By the time of Rinehart's death at eighty-two, the age of air travel and television were part of everyday life.

Today few people beyond the most avid mystery story fans know of Mary Roberts Rinehart. Yet through her life, she was a woman ahead of her time. At her death in 1958, she was internationally famous as a writer of over three hundred mystery stories, plays, movie scripts, articles, and works of serious fiction. A public person who counted presidents and cabinet members and giants of industry among her close friends, she had also become a woman of substantial means.

But in earlier years, life for her father and mother, Tom and Cornelia Roberts, and their two daughters, Mary Ellen and Olive, was an economic battle, sometimes not far removed from real poverty. Hard work was a way of life. Even her marriage to Dr. Stanley Marshall Rinehart in 1896 brought little relief from the need to watch every penny. But in 1904 she began to sell her stories and soon her fortunes changed and changed rapidly.

By 1910 she was earning fifty thousand dollars a year. A year later the family moved into an elegant home in Pittsburgh's most fashionable suburb of Sewickley. From then until her death, her prodigious output of work allowed her to live in a grand manner even she might not have imagined possible.

At thirty-four, she was a professional success. But always she was torn between duty to her husband and her three sons, her writing, and the public life she loved. She struggled to balance it all; and, like women today, she frequently paid the price. Her health failed. In all, she underwent surgery fifteen times, once for breast cancer. She was plagued with guilt over leaving her aging mother by herself more often than she should have. Her marriage was tested to the limit.

In her autobiography, *My Story,* she revealed that "I inherited from my mother a sort of fierce driving energy and a practical outlook on life. . . . But such invention as I have, such dreams as I have dreamed have come from my father." Occasionally, characters in her novels were assigned some of her own qualities as in the case of the protagonist, Elizabeth June who appeared in a story written in 1941. "She was a sensible woman . . . a person with good character, an essentially fair person and with a fund of humor. She was not a person content to be simply an onlooker."

A writer first, Mary also cared deeply about and carefully observed the world around her. In the early days of the first World War, the United States held to its neutral position as the German army swept through Belgium into France. Mary was certain the American people needed to know the facts from a woman's point of view, and she persuaded the publisher of the *Saturday Evening Post* to send her to the war front.

Six months later, her trip to Glacier National Park in 1915 triggered her fascination with the West. Her interest never flagged; and in 1929 when President Herbert Hoover asked her to serve on the newly established Commission on Conservation and Administration of the Public Domain, she readily accepted.

With the onslaught of the Second World War, she longed to be near the front lines, reporting the action, but instead she found herself on the Advisory Council of the Writers' War Board. Along with Thornton Wilder, Elmer Rice and Edna Ferber, she wrote countless pieces supporting the war effort. Yet restless with what she once called "this bosh," she also became an air raid warden.

Age and a serious heart condition finally began to take their toll. Still, she continued to write. She had become an institution, sought after for interviews, and the recipient of numerous awards. In 1954 she was presented a special award by the Mystery Writers of America for her outstanding achievements and for the great number of successful crime novels she had written.

Mary Roberts Rinehart died on September 22, 1958.

Chapter One

Mary Roberts hardly dared breathe as she waited in Dr. Willard's small reception room. For the first time in her life, her brown hair was out of braids and pinned on top of her head. She had taken the tuck out of the hem of her pink and white dimity dress so that it almost touched the floor. She wore her best hat, white with pink roses. Beside her was a rose-colored parasol. On her nose was a light dusting of face powder. She desperately wanted to look grown up, for it was essential to make the right impression.

Glancing up at the clock on the wall, she felt a flick of annoyance. It seemed that she'd been waiting for hours. Suddenly, the door to the office opened and she tensed. A head appeared, thick-haired, a small mustache, dark eyes, with pince-nez balanced on the bridge of the nose. Then the man himself stepped out. It was not Dr. Willard.

"Are you waiting to see Dr. Willard?" he asked briskly as if he was in a hurry.

She rose. "Yes, I am."

"Well, I'm taking his place this summer." He stepped to one side of the door. "Won't you come in?"

[1]

"No. No, thank you. You see, I'm not sick or anything. I just wanted to ask Dr. Willard for some advice."

The man who seemed neither young nor old gave her a kind of patronizing smile. "I'm Dr. Rinehart. Perhaps I could help."

There was something about this Dr. Rinehart that put her off. Maybe it was the pince-nez that made him look so stuffy. Still, she'd risked her mother's wrath to come here. And she'd been waiting for so long.

He pulled one of the chairs from across the waiting room and sat down. "Now, what's the problem?"

She eyed him warily, for an instant weighing whether she should talk to him, only to blurt out, "I want to be a nurse."

"I see," he said in seriousness. "Smoothing pillows and stroking fevered brows. That's the idea, isn't it?"

"Not at all," she said defiantly. "I can do whatever is necessary. I'm not afraid of work."

His glance took in her dress and parasol. "I can see that."

With every passing minute, she disliked him more. "Nursing is what I want to do."

She did not add that originally she had wanted to be a doctor. But she was only sixteen and would have to wait for two years before she would be eligible for medical school. Uncle John, who was always so generous with his good fortune, had offered to pay the tuition but it was impossible for her to wait that long.

"Have you ever considered teaching?"

"I don't want to be a teacher. Or a salesgirl, for that matter. But times are hard and I must help my family."

"And you've chosen nursing to earn your way."

"Yes."

She had no patience for teaching and the world looked down on salesgirls. Nursing was the solution. Though Mother considered it even lower in social status than a clerk, Mary was sure it was the right course for her to take.

Last summer, thousands of men all over Pittsburgh were thrown out of work by the terrible Homestead strike in the steel mills. At the same time, banks were failing and farm

"For the first time in her life, her brown hair was out of braids and pinned on top of her head. . . . She desperately wanted to look grown up, for it was essential to make the right impression."

mortgages were foreclosed. The entire country was gripped by a terrible depression. Father's only choice was to go out on the road to sell soft drinks and wallpaper.

Their family had never been rich. Far from it. But Father and Mother had given both her and her sister Olive bicycles before many other girls had them. And she had piano lessons. But one day all that had changed.

She recalled the strange feeling she had the moment she closed the front door behind her that afternoon. The house seemed too quiet. She climbed to the second floor and as she glanced down the hall, she noticed her belongings neatly stacked outside Olive's door. Puzzled, she went upstairs to her room and turned the handle. But the door was locked.

Her mother must have heard her for she appeared, needle-work in hand, from what was the maid's room when they could afford one. "Your room's been rented," she said, matter-of-factly.

"Oh," was all Mary could think to say and she had turned to go back downstairs. But step by step, the humiliation of taking in roomers grew. She could never again face her friends.

Tears brimmed in her eyes and by the time she had reached the ground floor she almost failed to notice the parlor door was open. Except on special occasions, Mother kept the parlor sealed off from casual visitors who might damage the cherished furniture she had scrimped and saved to buy. Mary had walked in on tiptoe and saw a barren room. Not a stick of furniture remained—not Mother's rosewood piano, not the sofa, not the chairs. Mary gave a little gasp as she realized that it had been sold. Never could she complain about the roomers.

So when she finished high school in the spring, she had decided to do something to add to the family coffers. But it had to be something out of the ordinary, away from home and Allegheny. She had to strike out on her own.

"Look, Miss—" she heard the formidable-looking doctor say.

"Miss Roberts. Mary Roberts."

"I have a suggestion, Miss Roberts. Maybe before you go any

[4]

further with this idea, you should see the hospital. I was an intern there. I could show you around."

"This afternoon?"

He raised his eyebrows. "I suppose I could. I'll lock up and get my hat."

As Mary waited for him to return, she could almost see the nurses in their starched uniforms, moving quietly from one bed to the next, the patients gazing up at them with grateful eyes.

Fifteen minutes later, Mary and Dr. Rinehart started off. The trolley rumbled out of Allegheny and over the Sixth Street bridge toward Pittsburgh. Several times Mary was on the verge of saying something to the austere man sitting beside her. But the right words didn't come to her and they silently stared out the window.

The day was hot and sticky and the soot-ladened air was already soiling her dress. At the proper street, Dr. Rinehart indicated it was their stop.

He pushed past the passengers standing in the aisle and stepped off the trolley. Mary struggled to follow and the closing door nearly caught her skirts as she jumped down to trot after him.

The street was lined with saloons and dilapidated houses in need of paint. At the end of the next block, they passed through a pair of immense gates and walked toward the front entrance of a large and gloomy red brick building with a sign that read: Pittsburgh Homeopathic Hospital.

They went through the heavy doors into the central hallway. It was dark and cool, and its wood floors gleamed like satin. Sounds were strangely muffled, the air full of a mixture of unfamiliar smells. At the end of the hall, she saw several shadowy uniformed figures moving quickly as they went about their business.

"This way. I want to introduce you to Miss Wright, the supervisor of nurses," Dr. Rinehart said.

A few moments later, Mary stood across the desk from a tall, erect woman. Her snow white hair was done in a fashionable pompadour and she wore a beautiful dress of black taffeta. Miss Wright might be the supervisor of nurses but she looked like a queen.

"Sit down, please." She indicated the chair next to her desk. "Dr. Rinehart tells me you wish to become a nurse."

Mary's heart pounded. "I do. Yes." She turned her head for some bit of assurance from Dr. Rinehart but he had left.

Miss Wright regarded her evenly. "Aren't you slightly young, Miss Roberts?"

She shook her head. "Oh, no. You see—"

"Exactly·how old are you?"

Her seventeenth birthday was in August, less than two months away. Studying her hands clutched around her purse, she told a white lie. Surely, God would not punish her, for a nurse was what she must become. She said, "I'm seventeen."

"And your next birthday?"

Mary gulped. "In August."

"Hmm," said the imposing lady thoughtfully as she continued to study Mary. "What you will see here at the hospital is often very unpleasant. It is life in the raw, you know."

"I'm willing to work, Miss Wright."

"That's good. Hard work is the backbone of the nursing profession. You do know that people die here at the hospital. In spite of all we can do."

Mary was certain Miss Wright was trying to discourage her but it wouldn't work. "I understand."

For a moment, Miss Wright drummed her long slender fingers lightly on the desk. "I don't know." Finally, she stood up. "All right. You may enter as a probationer. By the end of three months, we shall know if you have the stuff it takes."

Chapter Two

Mary returned home from the hospital, knowing her mother's opinion about nurses yet determined somehow to get her permission to enter the program.

That night as she stood next to her mother at the sink, drying the supper dishes, she carefully presented her argument.

"Mother, if you could only see Miss Wright. She's such a lady. Someone told me she's from one of the oldest families in Philadelphia."

With sleeves rolled up, her mother continued to attack the large pot she used for boiling potatoes.

"Mother—"

"I heard you, Mamie. And it doesn't make a bit difference. Nursing is beneath you."

"It's not beneath Miss Wright," Mary pressed.

"Each to his own," her mother snapped.

Mary eased the plate she had just dried on top of the others in the cupboard. "I want so to try."

"In spite of what I think?"

"Mother, please—"

Her mother straightened and eyed her with a look of exasperation. "You're a dreamer, Mamie. Just like your father. He sits around tinkering with those ridiculous schemes of his, thinking he's going to get a patent for them. And you're not a bit better. Dreaming that you're going to be some kind of Clara Barton. Well, nursing isn't like that. It's hard, filthy work. And I won't have my daughter doing it."

"If you saw the uniforms the nurses wear, Mother. There isn't a way in the world that anyone wouldn't respect a girl in that uniform."

"There's more to life than dress."

"When I get through with my training, I'll be paid eight dollars a month," she added, quietly.

"That much?"

Mary waited.

Her mother regarded her with tired eyes. Without a word, she untied her apron, hung it on a hook on the back of the door, and lowered the lamp.

She turned, and Mary followed her down the darkened hall to the foot of the stairs. With one hand on the newel post, Mother stopped and looked around at her.

"I don't approve, Mamie. I never will," she sighed. "But sometimes necessity gives us no choice."

Six weeks later—a day after her birthday—Mary packed her bag and set off for the Homeopathic Hospital. When Father returned home the Saturday after Mother had given her consent, he had merely raised an eyebrow, shrugged in what Mary thought was acceptance, and returned to reading his book. Perhaps he had been relieved that there would be one less mouth to feed.

Now, as she strode across the courtyard and tried to push back her nervousness, a black doorman came toward her and took her bag.

She followed him inside and down the hall. She decided that he must be very old, for he was stooped and his hands were gnarled. His black face was lined and puckered. But when he turned back to make certain she was behind him, his smile was so reassuring that in spite of her fright, she found the strength to smile back at him. Finally, they reached an open doorway and he turned in, pointed to a chair, set the bag down next to it and left.

Mary sat down. The blue foulard silk dress printed with tiny rosebuds and the wide-brimmed blue hat she wore were her Sunday best. Inside the carpetbag was little beyond three cotton print dresses and three aprons Mary and her mother had made of handkerchief linen. Probationers, she'd been told, were not issued uniforms.

She clasped her hands together to try to keep them from shaking and perspiration beaded along her upper lip. The air was heavy with the odor of iodine, and she heard people hurry up and down the hall.

A slender young woman came into the room. Her starched uniform crackled as she moved. The heels of the smallest shoes Mary had ever seen clicked against the wood floor.

"Mary Roberts?"

She stood and tried to smile.

"I'm Miss Leonard, the Assistant Supervisor. I'll take you to your room and you can get settled."

The room was on the top floor, the third door on the left from the elevator. The ceiling was high. Through the lone window, Mary could see roof tops etching the late day's opaque sky. The white walls were bare of decoration. The meager size of the room barely accommodated the four narrow beds—the first indication that she was to have roommates—the two bureaus, a small writing table, and several chairs. There was as yet no sign of anyone else's belongings.

"Supper is at five o'clock in the dining room," Miss Leonard informed her, and vanished through the door.

Mary slowly let her bag down on the floor and walked over to the open window. Below was a courtyard paved with cement. The hospital loomed up around it on three sides. In the corner was a stable. Beyond the gate came the noisy bustle of the city. She moved over to one of the beds and gingerly sat down.

It seemed impossible that this afternoon she could have

deliberately stepped inside this strange world. She was nobody. People walked past her as if she was invisible. She had left Pine Street only four hours ago and she was already filled with loneliness.

How brave she had felt, kissing Mother and her little sister Olive good-bye. How uncertain and scared she was now. She drew in a long breath, desperate to think of something that might raise her spirits.

What about all those others who had set out to conquer new worlds? The knights in the Crusades. The dashing explorers who set off across uncharted seas. Or the woman doctor on her very own street. None of them had stayed safely at home. Nor had she. She stood up and smoothed her dress.

The moment she stepped out into the hallway, the aroma of food pointed the way to the dining room. Though only a few minutes after five when she walked in the large room, it was already crowded. Nurses sat on either side of long tables. Interns in their white starched jackets with brass buttons were off to themselves. Everyone was talking, but not to her.

Self-conscious in the blue dress that she had put on so proudly this morning, she looked about and noticed several nurses standing by a steam table, waiting to be served. She walked over to join them and smiled a hello. But only a mildly curious glance was sent her way as the young women continued their conversation. When she finally sat down with her tray of food, it was all she could do to stab dejectedly at the piece of pork on her plate. Not even the pie was appealing.

It was barely past six when she returned to her room. She left the door open in hopes of getting some air, and sat down in the straight-backed chair to watch the night nurses file down the hall, strangely quiet in their shoes padded with bandages.

After a while, she closed the door, undressed, pulled on her cotton nightdress, and lay down. In the growing dark, she stared up at the high ceiling, afraid of failing, determined to try, and already homesick. A welcome drowsiness began to overtake her and she prayed for help in the days ahead.

Suddenly, someone was pounding on the door and she sat

up, blinking at the grey dawn beyond the window. She must have slept but her head felt as if it was stuffed with cotton. The door opened and Miss Leonard peered in.

"You are to report to Ward E at seven," she said brusquely and closed the door.

Mary stared after her. She had no idea where Ward E was and in the meantime, she must wash and dress and get what breakfast might be provided. All without so much as a single friendly hand or encouraging smile.

For a moment, she hunched over her crossed legs, head down, filled with her misery. And then slowly, she began to get angry. No one was going to make her give up. Certainly, not yet. She'd get to Ward E, wherever it was, and on time. But what on earth she was to do once she got there, she had not the slightest idea.

An hour later, Mary stood at the entrance of Ward E. The women's typhoid ward. For as long as she could remember, typhoid had descended across the city every year when the summer heat had dried the rivers until their banks were cracked mud and their swift flowing water turned to sluggish streams.

The room was large and long with windows on both sides. Under the windows was a double row of beds with white iron frames and high off the floor. Fifteen in all. Hooked onto the foot of each was a card that described the patient and the nature of her illness. In the center of the aisle between the beds was a round table covered with a bright red cloth. What little space was left was filled with cots. Every bed, every cot, was full.

The head nurse took Mary aside and explained that she was to bring bed pans to the patients when needed, empty them and wash them clean. She was to make beds and take away the dirty bed linen. There were floors to polish and window sills to be kept free of soot. She was to bathe the patients and fine comb their hair for lice. Mary felt herself flag as she listened to the list of duties and decided that whatever menial jobs there were in the hospital, probationers must do them. Still, she was here and she pushed back her dread. It was time to begin.

Before her were two dozen sick women, some almost skeletons, some out of their heads with delirium, some recovering. Two nurses and one probationer—Mary—were to care for them all. Without knowing what she was doing and full of uncertainty, she began.

One by one, beds were changed. Each patient's hair was combed, examined for lice and braided. Each patient was bathed. Their mouths were cleansed and searched for fever sores. Clumsily at first but soon expertly, Mary fed those who could not feed themselves.

The first time Mary emptied a bedpan, she retched. The first patient she bathed, she nearly closed her eyes for she had never seen a naked body other than her own. Her pride ached with the humiliation of the tasks. Her mother might have been right after all. Perhaps nurses were no better than servants. But in her heart, she would not let herself believe it and she steeled herself to get through the day.

Finally, twelve hours later, her duty was over. Only evening prayers remained before supper and then, blessedly, bed.

Feeling the outsider, Mary stood at the back of the small room that served as a chapel. As she watched the nurses file in slowly, their faces drawn in exhaustion, their caps awry, their aprons blood-stained, she felt a hand on her shoulder and she looked around. It was the head nurse of Ward E.

"You did very well today," she said quietly.

Miss Leonard called for prayer and everyone kneeled before their hard oak chairs. For an instant, Mary hesitated. Kneeling was not part of being a Presbyterian. Still, she must do what was expected. Awkwardly, she went to her knees and bowed her head.

"Almighty and most merciful Father, we have erred. . . ." She felt the prayer working its magic healing. She recalled the encouraging words of the head nurse like a salve on her bruised spirit. She made a silent pledge that she would be the very best nurse the hospital had ever seen.

When the prayers were over, she pushed herself up and made her way wearily back to her room to find it cluttered with luggage. Obviously, her roommates had arrived. But she was too exhausted to be even civil and she went to bed.

Chapter Three

The next afternoon, Mary was sent to the operating room to clean up. Visions of a floor awash with blood filled her head and it was all she could do to continue walking down the hall.

As she approached the double doors, Mary saw Jean Nelson, one of her roommates and a fellow probationer, waiting for her.

The girl's hair was flame red and so thick the pins barely held it on top of her head. The heavy white apron she wore made her look even thinner than she was.

They exchanged nervous smiles. Neither of them made a move to go into the amphitheater.

"Do you think you'll get sick?" Jean whispered, her face already chalky.

"I hope not."

They continued to stare at the double doors for a moment until finally Mary said, "Oh, come on. Maybe it won't be as bad as we think." And she went inside.

The operating room was an amphitheater. In the tiled well was the operating table, the glass topped instrument tables, the white and glass cabinets containing other instruments. A semicircle of seats rose all around. A great electric dome hung over the operating table, lighting the room.

Mary gazed about her. Disorder was everywhere. Towels in wads on the wet floor. Blood-stained sheets bunched on the operating table. Instruments strewn on the glass-top tables. Pans floating with dark red liquid. Two nurses worked busily by a box hissing with steam, which was mounted on long metal legs. One of them looked up and motioned to the girls.

"Over there," the nurse said to Mary. "Take that pail out and empty it."

"Yes, m'am." She looked in the direction of the operating table. From here, it seemed to be no more than an ordinary pail.

But when she leaned down to grasp the handle, she almost fainted, for there in the bottom was a human foot. Bile rose in her mouth. Somehow she swallowed it down, picked up the pail, and dumped the contents in a bin provided for such items in the back room. Lightheaded from the shock, she paused before going back into the amphitheater and wondered what else was in store for her.

Once inside, she saw Jean trying to lift a large rubber sheet encrusted with blood; and Mary hurried over to help her.

"Nurse says we're supposed to wash it," Jean said.

Mary took one end and they managed to drape it across a table.

"Do we use soap and water?" she whispered to Jean.

The redheaded girl shook her head. "It's that stuff in the bottle there. Carbolic acid solution, nurse says."

Mary pulled out the stopper and carefully poured the liquid across the black surface. The air filled with the odor of a strong disinfectant, strong enough to sear her nostrils. She wondered if it would burn her hands. Gingerly, she and Jean took the brushes Nurse Evans had given them and began to scrub at the blood when suddenly Jean ran over to the window and gagged. It was several minutes before she returned, which left Mary to finish cleaning the sheet by herself. But it took the two of them to lift it over the railing of the amphitheater where it might dry.

Mary glanced at her new friend who was as pale as her apron. "Are you all right?" she asked.

Jean nodded, looking sheepish. "I think it was the chloroform."

"Maybe so," agreed Mary, though she knew there was no chloroform in use. She was grateful for a strong stomach.

By the time they were finished, the operating room was spotless. The instruments that the nurses had sterilized and rubbed dry with pumice shone as they lay arranged in neat order in the glass-front cabinets. The saws and scissors were small but deadly looking. The glass-top instrument tables glistened. Everything was clean and in its place. Mary gazed about her filled with a strange sense of satisfaction. She had survived her first real test.

The rest of the week was no easier. The nights remained stifling and often Mary went up to the roof with the nurses to get a breath of air. Below on the roofs of the surrounding buildings lay men and women and children, some sprawled perilously near the edges. As she gazed at the grotesque shapes, Mary struggled to remember what it was like to live in a neighborhood, even one as poor as this one. She had been here for only a week yet it seemed a lifetime.

The truth was that for her there was no going home. It was only her seventh night at the hospital, yet she felt like an entirely different person. She was dropping off her former self like an animal shedding its skin. Now her concerns went far beyond the petty neighborhood jealousies or the price of meat at Mr. Kaufmann's butcher shop. She did not ever wish to go back.

She would never allow herself the humiliation of depending on someone else for her existence like some of the women her mother and grandmother whispered about. Like slaves, the roof over their heads, their clothing, the very food they ate came from someone else. More certainly than she had ever known anything, she was determined that wretched existence would never be hers.

Finally, she went back downstairs and eased onto the edge of the narrow bed to soak her aching feet and practice taking her own pulse. Jean Nelson and Lila Goodnow, her newest roommate, were both on night duty. With the air pressing down like a great blanket, she lay back to fall into an exhausted sleep.

Day by day, the newness and the initial terror subsided. She began to think for herself. She began to realize that behind the orderly rows of labeled bottles, linen rooms stacked with sheets and towels, endless shining floors, and lines of beds were people. Poor people. Desperately poor. Only a few could pay the six dollars a week that would guarantee that a napkin was placed on their meal trays.

There were men with arms gone who could never again lift great weights in the mills and who knew no other kind of work. A child who had his hand severed in a laundry begged her to have the doctor sew it back on. Girls no older than she, prostitutes knifed and beaten by customers, were carried in, their feet thickly calloused because they had never owned shoes.

Sometimes, when the day seemed to overflow with misery, the tragedy these men and women and children were forced to bear was almost too much for her. But there were still bacteriology and anatomy classes to attend and then, finally, sleep.

She already knew that to dwell on the injustices created by mill owners who cared nothing for the men who worked for them and on mere children faced with supporting their families was useless. Work was her salvation.

Every morning, Davy, the night watchman, would pound on the door.

"Six o'clock," he called. Waking the sleeping girls was the last chore of his watch.

For Mary and Jean and Lila and for the other nurses, the day was only beginning. The heat was fraying tempers and this morning when she entered the ward, the head nurse motioned to her impatiently.

"Bed five will need a screen," she said brusquely and walked away.

Mary remembered the patient in bed five. She was close to her age, maybe fifteen, so thin her legs were no more than sticks and the skin of her face was stretched taut and sallow from years of near starvation. But when Mary had brought her water or brushed her hair, the girl always smiled up at her in gratitude.

Mary put the screen around the unconscious girl. But as she stepped back, she caught a glimpse of the card clipped to the foot of the bed. On the line where the name of the patient's nearest friend was to be notified, nothing was written. The girl was to die completely alone.

Mary moved slowly down the aisle between the beds. She glanced at the head nurse and the two student nurses. There they were: calmly speaking to patients, taking temperatures, administering medicine as if nothing unusual was happening. It was as if they didn't care about the girl behind the screen.

"Can't you see this girl is alone and dying?" she wanted to cry. But instead, she went back to fold the sheets.

The day wore on. It was late afternoon when an intern came into the ward and went behind the screen. A moment later, he emerged and beckoned to the head nurse to join him. Only a few moments passed before they reappeared and hurried off. Soon two orderlies entered the ward carrying a stretcher.

Mary was feeding an elderly patient and tried not to look. Finally, the screen was removed. And along with all the patients, Mary watched as the girl was carried out, neatly covered by a sheet.

She glanced at the woman she was feeding. Her face was blank of any emotion as if death was an ordinary occurrence in her life. Mary looked down the row. Not a tear or a sorrowful expression anywhere. The girl—unknown—was gone and they were still alive, like a terrible contest that they had won.

Mary hurried over to remove the bedding and the mattress. Everything had to be sterilized. She went into the supply closet to get replacements. Coming back out, her arms full of linens to make up the bed, she looked at the student nurse and the two registered nurses—one of them the head nurse—as they moved about with quiet efficiency. These three women were expected to care for twenty patients. There was too much to be done to allow themselves the luxury of reacting to every death. Or so she kept telling herself. Somehow she must convince herself that their detachment was like the angels in Heaven who kept the Great Record. But she wasn't sure she could.

Yet she knew that life was for the living; and slowly, each woman who survived became important to her. Sometimes as she passed their beds, they would catch at her sleeve to hold her back, to tell her about their children or their own childhoods.

One day, an old lady in a corner bed beckoned to her. Mary smiled and went on making another bed.

"Nurse," the woman hissed.

Mary looked up. The woman beckoned to her again with a knobby finger and she went over to see what she wanted.

"Ya've been a dear to me, that ya' have. Kind as me own mother," she whispered. "So I want ya' to have somethin'." She glanced about her to make certain the woman in the next bed was not watching and then reached into her nightstand. For a moment, she rummaged in its contents until she drew out a well-worn coin purse. Holding it close to her, she carefully removed a quarter and handed to Mary.

"It's fur bein' so good, do ya' see." The woman's rummy eyes misted.

Mary gazed down at the coin in her hand. "Oh, Mrs. Delaney. I couldn't. Really."

The woman reached out and patted her arm. "No, no. It's fur ya', dearie."

Hesitantly, Mary slipped the coin into the pocket of her apron. "Thank you," was all she could say.

The rest of the afternoon she was able to think of nothing else. She could not keep the money. What in the world could she do? And then after supper, she approached Davy and asked him to buy her some oranges.

"How many d'ya want?"

"As many as a quarter will buy," she said. "And, Davy, could you do another favor?"

He gave her a crooked grin. "Name it."

"If I gave you another dime, could you wrap them somehow? You know. So they'd be like a present. And bring them up to Ward D."

He shrugged in a good natured way. "Don't see why not. But a present for who?"

Mary smiled and said, "They're for Mrs. Delaney in bed eighteen."

"Ah, you're a sweetheart, you are," he said.

She tried to smile but she was too tired. She knew every small kindness was important but there were so many lonely women in that ward. The thought of their desperate straits overwhelmed her. And she wondered how she would ever get used to it.

Chapter Four

T hree months to the day since she had followed the doorman through the front entrance, Mary received a message from
Miss Wright to go down to her office.

"Roberts, we have watched you carefully."

"Yes, m'am."

"On the whole, we believe you have done reasonably well."

Mary held her breath. "Reasonably well" was not the same
as "very well" or "exceptionally well." She tensed, nervous
about what was to follow.

"Yes, m'am."

"You've had the opportunity, though brief, to see how demanding the profession of nursing is." Miss Wright leaned
forward, resting her elbows on the desk, and surveyed her
solemnly.

Mary's heart pounded. Why didn't the Supervisor just come
out and say her training days were over?

"Yes, m'am." She tried to keep her voice steady and steel
herself for the worst.

Miss Wright suddenly rose and with a smile walked around
the desk to take her by the hand. Mary pulled herself up very
straight and fixed a brave smile on her face, the smile she used

when life didn't work out the way she wanted it to. "So, Miss Roberts," the Supervisor said, "I am happy to tell you that you have been officially accepted into the student nursing program of the Homeopathic Hospital of Pittsburgh."

Mary blinked, but said nothing.

"I said you were accepted into the nursing program."

"Oh, my." Mary took in quick breath in her astonishment. "Oh, thank you. Thank you."

Mary wanted to hug this tall woman, but instead she tried to match her dignity and as calmly as she could she added, "I promise you I will do my very best."

Today Mary wore the uniform of a student nurse: blue and white striped with a white Eton collar and a little white tie. Around her waist was a heavy, wide-belted apron. The skirt was two inches above the floor. The cap of stiff tulle, pleated into a narrow band, she placed exactly on the top of her head.

From her belt hung a black bag for her curved surgical scissors, dressing forceps, and thermometer. She was to receive a salary of eight dollars a month but student nurses were required to supply their own thermometers and Mary suspected that by the end of the month little of the eight dollars would remain. Miss Leonard had told her she was to report to the operating room.

As she walked down the hall, she noticed two doctors talking. One of them she recognized as Dr. Rinehart. She had seen him on a number of occasions, but always at a distance. When she passed him now, he glanced her way and smiled.

It was against all the rules for doctors and nurses, especially student nurses, to speak except on matters connected with patient care. Besides, Dr. Rinehart was famous for a fierce temper. And last June, he had not impressed her as particularly pleasant. Even if there was no rule against it, she could think of nothing she wanted to say to him.

With a brief nod and a perfunctory smile, she put him out of her mind for she was already fearful about what lay ahead in the operating room.

She pushed open the door to the anteroom and changed into the customary garb: a long, straight white gown with short sleeves and mob-cap, grey white from countless sterilizations, to cover her hair. The effect was unbecoming, no matter who wore the costume. In a cubicle lay the patient—a boy of thirteen or so. After scrubbing her hands, she went into the operating room. The Supervisor was in charge of preparations and Mary hurried over to her.

"What is it, Miss Wright?"

"Amputation. S.M. will be operating. I'll show you the solutions he'll want and the cat gut he uses."

Mary nodded. "S.M." was hospital shorthand for Stanley M. Rinehart to distinguish him from his brother who also practiced here. For some reason, it had never occurred to her that she might find herself working with the man who not minutes ago had smiled at her. Plainly, to see him in the hall was one thing. To stand behind him at the operating table was quite different.

At the moment, though, she must help the other nurses fill the irrigators and get out the instruments. She could not keep her hands from shaking. It was Dr. Rinehart who had helped her to come here and yet what if, on this very first day as a student nurse, she made some terrible mistake?

The patient, by now anaesthetized, was wheeled in. On his way to work in one of the mills, the boy had slipped crossing an icy street and been crushed by a streetcar. Mary glanced at the young face so innocent now in sleep and tried not to think of his life with only one leg.

Dr. Rinehart suddenly appeared and came to the operating table. He asked the supervisor several questions and set about the operation. Never once did he turn around. He did not even see Mary. All her worry was wasted.

Yet she was glad she was here. Now S.M. was more than a slightly disagreeable man who wore pince-nez. She had seen him totally absorbed in his work. Nothing distracted him. The operation had gone smoothly so there was no cause for him to lash out at whatever nurse was at fault. She almost said a prayer of thanks. For she was the only junior nurse here today and the mistake probably would have been hers.

It was nearly Christmas. Though the other girls envied Mary because she was so close to home, she had been home only once since August. Even with Uncle John who had offered to send her to medical school, there was little she could talk about. How could she tell him of a human foot in a bucket or women delirious with fever screaming out obscenities or men with crushed arms and legs brought in from the mills? He would be concerned but would he understand her fright the first time during night duty when a patient died and she had to take him to the mortuary—a room off to itself, the gaslights playing queer shadows on the walls—where she had to bath him and clothe him in a shroud?

To learn of it would horrify the rest of her family. She was horrified. But she was learning to live with it. It was her special world, bounded by brick walls and a stable and brothels, in which her family had no part and never would.

So Christmas day began as every other day. Yet today the hospital seemed to be at rest. Mary was working in the men's ward. Each intern wore a sprig of mistletoe in the buttonhole of his white duck jacket. From the top floor kitchens came wonderful odors of roasting turkey.

At three o'clock, services were to be held in the chapel, and those patients like Roberto Filano, who could sit and move about, would attend. Mr. Filano was one of Mary's favorites. He had come from Milan to make his fortune. In the meantime, he worked at Carnegie's foundry where he had been blinded by flying debris from the blast furnace. Instead of self-pity, his words were full of cheer for the men in the beds around him. Now she wheeled him down the hall to the chapel.

Once she settled his wheelchair, Mary went to the old piano. Someone had told the Assistant Supervisor that she could play and a week ago Miss Leonard had asked Mary to take part in the Christmas program.

The other nurses in crisp caps and fresh uniforms sat in the

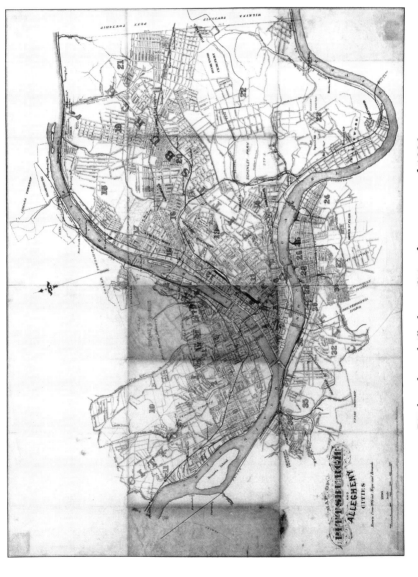

Pittsburgh and Allegheny Cities, from a map of 1890.

first three rows. Interns lounged against the back wall, ready to dash out if there was an ambulance call. She adjusted her chair and had begun to glance through the music book when she became aware of someone standing by her side. She looked up.

Dr. Rinehart smiled at her. "I've been asked to lead the singing," he explained. "What do you think, Nurse Roberts? What should we start with?"

His eyes were warm, friendly. She returned his smile. "How about 'Oh, Little Town of Bethlehem'?"

"Perfect." He stepped forward and the undertone of conversation stilled. Glancing back, he asked quietly, "Shall we begin?"

Dr. Rinehart's rich baritone filled the room. Soon everyone was singing. Pale winter sunlight filtered through the stained-glass window and spread across those gathered. As Mary played, any bit of loneliness she had felt earlier in the day evaporated.

That night, Mary was scheduled for duty and would be in charge of three wards and the emergency ward. As always, she was terrified that during the long night something would happen that she could not handle. And she knew the dangers that lurked in the waning hours of the night, when she was desperate for sleep. She must keep walking, moving, doing anything, for the moment she sat down she might fall instantly asleep.

It was nearly midnight. The gaslights had been turned low and the darkened wards stretched like great caves from the dim light near the door. At the moment, the convalescing patients in Ward E were resting quietly. Most were asleep. As she moved down the hall to the next ward, she glanced out the window patterned with frost. Snow muffled the shouts and laughter from the saloons and the brothels across the street. A lone carriage waited at the curb for a customer, and the breath of the horse smoked out in a steamy cloud.

She turned away and was entering Ward C when she heard

the bells of the ambulance. She tensed, knowing another patient was about to come into the emergency ward. She hurried downstairs.

The doors to the emergency entrance swung open to reveal a burly policeman, well over six feet tall. Tears were coursing down his face as he carried in his arms a newsboy, no more than seven or eight years old, his skin and hair blackened with burns.

"The boy was only tryin' to warm himself," the great bear of a man explained as he laid his charge gently down on one of the two beds covered with gray blankets. "It's fierce cold out there tonight. He was buildin' a bit of a fire but somethin' went wrong."

The child's breath was labored. As gently as they could, Mary and the intern cut away the charred clothing. Pieces of skin stuck to the fabric, leaving raw wounds.

"I'll need gauze and tannic acid. And morphine."

"Yes, doctor."

The policeman hovered nearby. "How's the boy to heal?" he asked in a hushed tone.

"If he makes it through the next few hours, he'll need skin grafts. His own skin is best but for now other people's will have to do." The intern shook his head. "In fact, with the extent of the burns, he'll need skin from several people."

"I'll get 'em, doc. One way or another, I'll get 'em." And the policeman wheeled and disappeared down the hall.

Mary and the intern did what they could to clean the boy. With utmost care, the young doctor poured tannic acid solution over the wounds and covered them lightly with strips of gauze.

"He'll need all the liquids you can get down him, Roberts."

"Yes, doctor."

For the first time since the boy had been brought in, his eyes opened. Dazed with the excruciating pain that even the morphine failed to disguise, they stared up at Mary as if begging her to help him.

"There, there. You'll be all right, child," she said softly. Her heart wanted to believe it. She wanted the boy to believe it. But her brain told her that unless a miracle occurred he would be dead by morning.

The hours went on. Mary moved quickly between the wards and the emergency room. Two more people were brought in: a man with stab wounds and another who had taken an overdose of drugs, attempting suicide. Desperation was at the root of both emergencies, for the Depression had pushed hundreds of men out of work. She thought of her own father, barely eking out a living for his family. He talked of his patents, of how any day someone would buy one of his ideas and their life would take a turn for the better.

Still, Mary had never starved, though she could pinch a penny till it squeaked. And for as long as she could remember, the rule of the day at the Roberts's house was to cut corners. But she thanked God she knew nothing about the poverty that drove people to such total despair.

Mary hurried back to the second floor to check the other wards. Behind a screen in the men's ward a patient lay near death. His forehead was clammy, his pulse slow, his breathing erratic. By sunrise, he would be dead. Someone should sit by his side, be with him in his last hours. But she had no time. At least he's unconscious, she thought wearily. And she adjusted the sheets over his shoulders and left.

Downstairs again, she went to check on the newsboy. Automatically, she took his slender wrist between her fingers and began to check his pulse when she felt a touch on her arm.

"Little nurse," a deep voice said and she looked up to see the policeman. Behind him were three priests.

Their unlined faces and slim figures suggested that two were in their mid-twenties. The third was grey-haired. His cassock failed to hide a potbelly. He spoke. "We've come for the boy here."

"I beg your pardon?"

"Officer McElvey says the boy needs skin grafts."

"He does. But—"

"Shall I get the doctor?" the hulking policeman asked, anxiously.

"No, no. I'll call him."

Within minutes, the intern appeared with a dressing gown over his pajamas, his hair uncombed, his eyes sagging with sleep. He looked at the three priests uncertainly.

"You know what the procedure involves?" he asked.

"I'm Father Ruensa, doctor," the older priest said. "I presume you will remove a piece of our skin and give it to the child."

"Right. But it's not exactly like cutting off a lock of your hair."

"I realize that."

"It's damn painful."

"As painful as it is for the boy there?" the grey haired priest asked quietly.

"Not quite." He slid back the boy's eyelids and examined his eyes. "He's having a first rate fight of it. Frankly, Father, I don't know if it's worth it."

The two men stood side by side, gazing down at the child.

"We're both in the business of saving lives, doctor."

"So we are," observed the exhausted intern. "So let's get at it."

Mary and the intern scrubbed their hands with a solution of carbolic acid. The priests rolled up their sleeves. Mary swabbed each man's arms with alcohol.

Father Ruensa volunteered to be first. With the pincers of a hemostat, the doctor carefully lifted the skin on the priest's forearm until the skin was the shape of miniature tent the size of a large quarter. Next he took a scalpel and made an incision around the diameter. Deftly, he cut the skin away from the tissue. The priest paled. The piece of skin was placed on a raw section of the boy's chest and covered with a strip of gauze.

Mary bandaged the priest's arm. "Are you all right, Father?" she asked.

"It's not me you need worry about."

Immediately, the first of the two younger men took his place. The procedure was repeated. At last, the third man took a seat by the bed. Like the other priests he never moved or cried out in pain but his color was bad, almost green. Mary gently secured the gauze around his arm. As he stood to leave, his knees buckled and he fell to the floor unconscious.

The intern glanced up from his work with the boy. "Roberts, get the good father some fruit juice and have him lie down for a while. And then come back here to give me a hand."

Chapter Five

Mary stretched out on her bed, her feet and legs swollen as usual from the hours of standing, and stared up at the high ceiling. Across the room, Lila Goodnow snored softly. Two floors below a child clung to life. The man in Ward C had died before she went off duty. But earlier in the week, eighteen men and women had died in one night. By comparison, last night had been quiet.

She closed her eyes. In the first weeks of training, she had promised herself to keep a record of all this: to write about everything and everyone. But the long hours and the horror around her took its toll. After a dozen false starts, she had put her pencil and pad aside. How could she find the words to describe the slender priest who had silently crumpled to the floor? Or the hardened policeman weeping? Or the emaciated corpse she had washed and dressed for burial earlier this morning?

Words brought back the feelings of despair and the pain. Some day, she might be able to view it all objectively but not now.

Now she must force herself to shut out the noises of the new day and gather her strength for the night to come. She mustn't even allow herself to stay awake to think of Dr. Rinehart who had approached her in the hall outside the dining room this morning.

"Still holding out, I see," he had said, pleasantly.

"Of course," she had answered, for it was true. She was too tired to play games. Two other nurses moved past her. Their faces were void of any expression but their eyes danced at the sight of a forbidden association going on in broad daylight. She had met their stares and then suddenly she began to feel a certain thrill at what she was doing—standing here before God and everyone else, talking with a physician.

With a surge of bravado, she had added, "In fact, I was thinking about studying German and I wondered if perhaps you might have a book I could borrow."

His eyebrows had lifted, perhaps in surprise. "As a matter of fact, I think I do have a book. It's quite elementary. But it should be a good start. I'll leave it in your mailbox."

She had thanked him and they parted.

Now as she lay in bed, she wondered why she had brought up the subject of German to Dr. Rinehart. Most medical journals were written in German and in order to do her best in her classes, knowledge of German was important. But why in the world had she mentioned it to Dr. Rinehart? Her mind blurred with exhaustion. Later, she would figure it out.

But with the outbreak of smallpox in the hospital, even a moment to spend on personal reflection disappeared. The worst cases were sent to the Municipal Hospital. Extra nurses were needed and Mary volunteered to go with them but Miss Leonard told her she was too young. The patients left behind with only mild cases had to stay where they were until the quarantine was over. Mary was to stay with them. The doors were closed. Policemen were put on guard. No one could go in or out.

Some of the wards were empty, and these had to be disinfected. The windows were sealed. Bricks were piled in the center of a ward. A large pan was placed on the bricks and then another brick, red hot, went into the pan. Miss Leonard poured some powder onto the hot brick and then ran for the door. Mary and another nurse, who stood outside, slammed the door behind Miss Leonard and sealed it with wide strips of paper wet with flour paste.

In spite of every precaution, the acrid fumes seeped through the door and hung everywhere like a dreadful pall. Breathing was difficult. Appetites disappeared. And strangest of all, time which until now was so precious, seemed endless. Because no one could leave the hospital, there was no place to go except the roof or the courtyard. The patients grew restive. They threatened to march out of the hospital wearing nothing more than their gowns.

One afternoon an orderly wheeled the piano down to the ward from the chapel and Mary led an impromptu performance of singers from among the patients and staff. For a few hours, the strain eased.

But soon the tension began to build again. The night duty was the worst, for Mary imagined that in every shadow and behind every door lurked a rebellious patient, poised to spring out at her, grab her as a hostage, and demand his freedom.

The days were not much better. Patients eager to be released threw food and then chairs at the nurses and each other in their frustration. If one man thought a nurse had given another better treatment, a fist fight broke out.

After three weeks, the quarantine was lifted. And by that evening, the doctors who had been excluded moved through the halls once again.

Mary was standing at the night nurse's desk with its lamp and signal board, reviewing the patients' charts when suddenly she felt a light hand on her shoulder. "Did you get the book?" It was Dr. Rinehart.

"I—no, I didn't."

"I gave it to old Bill the doorman."

"He probably was ordered not to let anything in or out."

"Maybe so." His dark eyes smiled at her through the lenses of the pince-nez. "I'll see you get it tomorrow."

Instinctively, Mary glanced around to see if anyone was watching them as they talked. But the hall was empty.

"You know, it might help if we sat down and went over the pronunciation," he said. "After you've had a chance to go through some of the lessons, that is."

Her heart pounded. "It might."

"My office is on Second Street. And I live with my brothers on Western Avenue. We could meet at either place. On your day off."

His tone was very businesslike, matter-of-fact. But underneath it Mary thought she detected an amiable quality as if he thought they were already friends. Or perhaps more than friends.

Mary soon discovered that German was a total puzzle. Try as she might, she could make little sense out of the interminably long sentences and strange script. Still, she kept at it. Once or twice, after visiting her mother, she walked the few blocks to Dr. Rinehart's office where he attempted to show her how to roll her r's.

She found herself gazing at him as he read, transfixed by his clear sonorous voice.

After awhile, he looked up and asked, "Do you see how it goes now?"

Her chin in her hand, she nodded.

He raised an eyebrow. "You're sure?"

"Oh, indeed."

"Well, that's good. Because I'm not sure at all."

The slightly offhand way he said it made her wonder if he was joking. And yet, Dr. Stanley Rinehart was not known to joke.

"In fact—if you can keep a secret—it's like one huge labyrinth."

"You mean you don't think German is easy?" she asked.

"Do you?"

"Heaven's no. But I'm the student. And you're the teacher."

Suddenly, he burst out laughing. "Miss Roberts, you have a point."

After that another Stanley Rinehart appeared. He still shouted at any nurse who did not hand him an instrument quickly enough in the operating room. He did not tolerate mistakes. And he continued to affect the pince-nez. But she discovered that behind the austere little glasses was a warmth in the eyes that often twinkled at something he found funny. More than once, she saw how he treated the children in the pediatric ward with incredible kindness.

She and Stanley, as she now called him, began to meet at least weekly. Their talk was almost always of the hospital for it was the world they shared. By May, she decided it was time to introduce him to her family.

They sat, stiffly proper, in the parlor and watched as Mother poured tea.

"Sugar, Dr. Rinehart?" she asked with an uneasy smile.

"No, thank you, Mrs. Roberts."

Olive sat by the door to the front hall and stared at him in frank curiosity. Her father was on the road somewhere in southern Ohio.

Mary rose from her place on the settee next to Stanley and picked up the plate of cookies. "Another cookie?"

Stanley gave her mother his most engaging smile. "They're delicious. But I'm afraid not. Thank you."

Mother eyed Stanley over the rim of her tea cup. "You have your own practice then, Dr. Rinehart?"

"That's right. In fact, my office is not more than a block or two from Dr. Willard's."

"You don't say?" Mother shifted her glance to Mary and then back to Stanley.

"That's where Mary and I met, actually."

Her mother smiled and appeared to be a trifle more relaxed. The conversation turned to the warm weather and the hour wore on. Finally, thanks were offered and good-byes were said. Stanley had rented a rig and as they started off, neither of them spoke.

Mary suspected that Mother was duly impressed that a doctor

seemed to be romantically interested in her oldest daughter. It might have even lifted some of the onus from her nursing.

"Your mother is a fine woman," Stanley said finally.

"I know."

"Do you think she approved of me?"

Mary smiled at him. "Why on earth wouldn't she?"

But Stanley had turned his concentration to maneuvering the rig through the snarl of carriages and freight wagons as they converged at the entrance to the covered bridge spanning the Allegheny. Before long, they were able to move forward.

The light within the wooden casing of the bridge was dim and the air close, full of the smell of manure and horse hair. The rattle of wheels and the voices reverberated as Stanley guided the horse toward the other side. All at once, she felt his hand on hers. "Mary, what would you say if—"

She could barely hear him. "What?"

"I said what would you say if I asked you to marry me?"

All afternoon, she had sensed Stanley was leading up to the question so she wasn't surprised. Yet she still was unsure of what to say.

The carriage rolled out onto the street.

"Well?"

A trolley car clanged its bell at them and Stanley gave an impatient yank to the reins. In a moment, they were parked in front of a nearby warehouse.

"Oh, Stanley, I'm honored at your asking me."

"Hang the honor. Will you marry me?"

Mary thought of what Jean Nelson had said about him— about his temper and that she was a fool to go on seeing him. Jean certainly would disapprove of her marrying him. It was true about the temper. More important though was the fact that she wasn't sure she loved him.

"I don't quite know how to say this, Stanley—"

"Just say it," he urged.

"I like you. I like you a lot. But I'm not sure I love you."

Stanley smiled and took her hand. "Liking can grow to love awfully fast, Mary."

She glanced down at his hand on hers. "I know. But there's something else." She looked up into his brown eyes. "I want to graduate, Stanley. That's important to me. Probably the most important thing in my life."

"I understand."

"And I don't want to give up nursing."

"You wouldn't have to, Mary. Why, I'd depend on you once we were married. I'd need you to help me in the office every day."

She eyed him uncertainly. "You're not just saying that?"

He squeezed her hand. "No."

"Which means we can't be married for at least a year."

Stanley frowned, earnestly. "Are you saying 'yes'?"

She studied his face with its anxious expression. "I . . . I guess I am."

"Oh, Mary, that's wonderful." He reached out and hugged her to him.

The warmth of him and the strength of his arms around her was strange and exciting. But she wouldn't be eighteen for three months and even then maybe she wasn't ready to get married.

She pulled away from him. "I'm serious about graduating, you know."

"I realize that. At least we'll be engaged until then."

"How can we be? I mean, what if somebody at the hospital finds out?"

"And what if they do?"

"Why, they'll throw me out. That's what."

Stanley took her face in his hands and kissed her gently on the nose. "Just let them try it."

The following Saturday, Stanley paid a call on her parents to ask for her hand in marriage, they happily agreed and he presented her with a ring of small garnets and diamond chips. Though she knew she must hide it, the ring now made their engagement official.

With the gold circle dangling on a long ribbon around her neck and dressed in her blue foulard and matching hat, she was on her way downstairs a few weeks later to meet Stanley in the courtyard when suddenly he came striding through the front door. In a moment, he was by her side.

"I don't care if they found out," he announced to her sharply.

Mary stared at him. "What do you mean?"

"Somebody told Dr. Whitaker we were engaged."

"Oh, Stanley—"

"Never mind. I'm going in to see the Hospital Board now and we'll get the whole thing straightened out."

"But—" Mary began.

"You stay here. I'll be back in a few minutes."

As she peered over the railing, she could see the bearded and austere members of the Hospital Board march down the hall to disappear through the double doors of their meeting room on the first floor. She leaned back against the wall, not daring to guess what might be about to happen. The minutes went by. Angry voices drifted out into the hallway.

Mary moved to the balustrade again and looked down, one moment wishing Stanley had said nothing and the next minute bursting with pride over his bravery. The orderlies and nurses and interns eyed her without a word as they walked past, pretending to ignore the ruckus downstairs. For by now everyone could hear Stanley's rich baritone.

"I am telling you, gentlemen, that as long as I do my job and she does hers, what Miss Roberts and I do with our lives is our business only. We are engaged. We plan to be married at the end of her training. Her family has given their consent which is the only consent needed."

She strained to catch some fragment of the board's reply.

"I do not need your permission to take my fiancee driving. I came out of courtesy to Dr. Whitaker."

Mary heard the door open.

"And now if you will excuse me, Miss Roberts and I are leaving. I will return her to the hospital by six."

With weak knees, Mary started down the stairs. She was relieved that the matter of their engagement was out in the open now. But their marriage was still a year off. Ahead was what some nurses told her was the hardest part of the training.

Chapter Six

The last remainders of summer heat clung to the September days, drying the river bank mud into crevasses of never-ending designs. The season for typhoid was in full swing. It was the beginning of Mary's second year of training.

Now as a senior student nurse, she was expected to go out on private duty. The patients were too poor to pay the ten dollar charge that went to the hospital so it was usually paid by a fraternal organization. Secretly, she dreaded what she might face for she had heard all kinds of horror stories from the other nurses. Still, she knew the time would come soon and it did.

It was midnight when she was roused from bed by Davy and told to bring her bag. Not surprisingly, she was to nurse a woman with typhoid.

She walked briskly across the dimly lit courtyard toward Second Avenue and the darkened world beyond. In one hand she carried her little bag with a change of uniform, bandage scissors, bandage forceps, and her thermometer. Whiskey-rough laughter floated out of the open door of the saloon on the next corner. The sound of a tinny piano came from within the brothel across the street. A sliver of light shown out from between the curtains in a second floor window.

Two blocks down, the trolley suddenly swung around the corner and into sight and she hurried to the stop. By a rough guess, it would take her nearly a half hour to get to the address the Assistant Superintendent had scribbled on a sheet of paper.

In the nearly empty trolley, she chose a seat near the conductor and told him where she wanted to get off.

He peered around at her. "You're sure, miss? That's a bad part of town. And this time of night—"

"Someone's to meet me, I think."

"Oh, well then," he said, though his tone was still doubtful.

When the time came, she stepped down from the safety of the trolley into a street completely dark except for the feeble circle of light from the corner gas light. Suddenly, a man of medium height emerged from the shadows and came toward her.

She tensed. Was this man with several days growth of beard the person who was to meet her?

"Nurse Roberts?" he asked in a thick accent which she couldn't identify.

"I am. It's your wife who's ill?"

Without answering, he reached for her bag, turned and began to walk quickly down the street. She knew she'd been sent here to give comfort to a woman who probably would not live to see another day. But the man's wild eyes peering out at her from beneath his greasy cap frightened her. Visions of a house full of drunken characters filled her head. A nurse's uniform was not a guarantee against violence. But at this moment she had very little choice, and mustering all the courage she had within her, she trotted after him.

They walked single file for two blocks. Each house they passed was small frame, dilapidated, identical to its neighbor, and flush against the sidewalk with not even a patch of yard. Trash and bits of garbage lay against stairs and in corners.

In mid-block, the man stopped in front of one such house. He glanced back at her. "This way."

The room she entered was small and reeked of garbage and urine. Half a dozen men sprawled on the floor asleep, others with heads lolling on their chests were propped against the wall. All were barefoot.

The man motioned her to follow him up a steep flight of stairs to another room where several women sat on the floor. Two toddlers curled together in one corner. The air was stagnant and hot. Across the room was her patient, tossing on a mattress, wild with delirium.

Mary set her bag down by the sick woman and turned to the women who stared at her dumbly.

"You must leave."

They continued to stare at her. The woman on the bed suddenly screeched an obscenity.

"Out." Mary took one of the reluctant women by the arm and began to pull her toward the stairs. The woman tried to yank free but Mary held fast. "I mean it. Out. Right now."

One by one, the women slowly descended the stairs.

Mary forced the window open. In the dim light from the single lamp, she leaned over the patient to examine her. All the evidence told her the patient was close to death. The best she could do was to make her comfortable.

From the little she could learn from the other women, the patient's name was Anna. Her emaciated body was covered with sores. Her dark hair was matted and filled with lice. The sheets were filthy.

With the greying dawn, Mary went down to the kitchen where a bony girl stood hunched over the stove, her light brown hair hanging in strands around her gaunt face. Despite her haggard appearance, there was a certain childishness about her. Mary guessed she was no more than thirteen.

"I need hot water," Mary told her.

"Yes, miss," the girl whispered, shrinking away as she eyed Mary.

"And the sheets must be washed," Mary added.

"Yes, miss," she repeated.

"Is there coffee and something to eat?"

"Coffee, miss. A bit of bread's left, too."

Mary eased gingerly onto the chair next to the wooden table. The girl reached for a tin cup on the shelf above the stove and filled it with coffee. From a tin box, she drew a slab of bread and handed it to Mary.

"I keeps it in the box. 'Cause of the roaches," she explained.

"Oh, yes." Mary held the bread in one hand and took a tentative sip of the black liquid.

"See there, miss." The girl pointed to the leg of the table. "Have to be right quick or they'll eat the food right outa yer hands."

Mary jumped up, nearly spilling her coffee, and watched a cockroach scurry toward the bread crumbs. From the front of the house came the sound of the door opening.

"I must see the nurse," came a deep voice of authority.

Mary swung around. At the foot of the stairs was Dr. Campbell, an intern she recognized from the hospital.

"Dr. Campbell." She had seldom felt so relieved to see anyone in her life.

"Good morning, nurse. How's our patient?" he asked as she came closer.

"I don't think she'll last, doctor."

"Doesn't surprise me." He glanced up the stairs. "Come on. Let's take a look."

As Dr. Campbell straightened after his examination of the patient, he eyed Mary. "You want to go back to the hospital?"

"No, I'm fine, doctor."

"Anna Stefano isn't going to live past tomorrow. No matter what we do. Why don't you go back and get a good night's sleep?"

"Really. I'm fine."

"Look. I'll give the husband—if that's what he is—a powder for the poor soul. She'll rest comfortably—"

"No. I want to stay."

The dark-haired doctor shrugged. "Suit yourself." He took a few steps down the stairs. "But if you change your mind, send for me."

Mary nodded.

"Well, good luck," he said.

And a moment later the front door closed, leaving Mary alone with her dying patient. What she could do for the poor woman was relatively minor. Cooling baths. Fresh sheets. Broth. Little else. But that's what nursing was about: to serve the sick and helpless. And that's exactly what she intended to do.

The truth was that once her initial terror over this place and these people subsided, the challenge—and it was a challenge—of bringing some comfort to her patient and putting matters in the house to rights was strangely exciting, exhilarating.

By the end of the day, the only sheets were washed and dried and back on Anna Stefano's mattress. But her fever hovered around one hundred and three degrees and her pulse was slow. The foul ranting continued.

The woman had no reason to be alive but still she lingered. The third night of her stay, Mary sat in the rocking chair which someone had found and brought upstairs. Periodically, she rose to check her patient's pulse and temperature. Her shallow breathing began to falter. Then it rallied. Finally, it stopped altogether. Mary tiptoed downstairs to tell the woman's husband.

Her tap on his shoulder roused him. "I'm sorry to tell you, Mr. Stefano. Your wife is gone."

He stared at her dumbly, nodded, and promptly went back to sleep. Gazing down at him, she was stunned by his indifference. Yet it really didn't come as any surprise and as quietly as she could she mounted the stairs to return to her patient.

In the past year, Mary had prepared more men and women than she cared to remember for burial so she knew exactly what must be done. After bathing Mrs. Stefano and straightening her hair, she tied a length of bandage over her head and under her chin so that her jaw would remain closed. Finally, she propped up her head with several pillows so the blood would drain from her poor mottled face.

Satisfied, Mary sat down in the rocking chair to wait for daylight. In a moment, she was asleep.

Suddenly and with tremendous force, something jerked her backward and down onto the floor. Too frightened to cry out, Mary lay where she was for a moment. And then, fearfully, she glanced about her. She heard no one. How then had she been pitched to the floor? And then she saw it: Anna Stefano's body not two feet away, stiff with rigor mortis, lying across the rockers of the chair.

Mary gasped and staggered to her feet. She must have placed the body too close to the edge of the bed and as it stiffened it rolled off and across the rockers. Lightheaded with the horror of it, she could not seem to move as she stared down at the forlorn soul on the floor. Minutes passed. She knew what she must do. Still, she stood there. Finally, cringing, she leaned down to lift Mrs. Stefano back on the bed.

And then taking a deep breath, she straightened her uniform, adjusted her cap, and went downstairs to get the family.

To her relief, the number of typhoid cases waned. In November, she was assigned to go to a sanitarium in the mountains to bring a demented man back to the hospital. It was on the morning of their departure from the sanitarium that an orderly brought her a letter.

She stared at the envelope. The handwriting was her father's. In the nearly two years of training, she'd never once received a letter from him so why now? Her senses told her bad news lay inside and she hesitated to open it. But it was almost time to take her patient to the railway station so reluctantly, she tore off the end and slid out the single sheet of writing paper.

"Dear Mamie, It is with sadness that I must tell you of your grandmother's tragic death." The letter went on. Grandmother had caught her heel on a long dressing gown and fallen down a flight of steps, broken her neck, and died within hours. He told of the fine and useful life Grandmother had lived and that surely she was in Heaven.

Mary stood in the winter sunshine which filtered through the big window of sanitarium's front hall and read the letter over several times. The beauty of Father's words couldn't push aside the feelings growing inside her. Finally after all the years as a widow, eking out a living for her two sons, her grandmother was living in some comfort with her youngest daughter, Tillie. And then this had to happen? Where was the justice of such a needless death?

She longed to grab her bag and rush back to Pittsburgh. Yet the funeral already had been held. Grandmother was buried. Sadly, she tucked the letter in her pocket and went back to her patient to ready him for the train trip.

The days went by. When she wasn't sent out on a case, she was too busy in the hospital to grieve. Occasionally, she saw Stanley which helped to ease her feelings. And then less than two weeks later, an orderly brought her a telegram.

This time there were no soothing words. Only a short sentence. It was from Aunt Tillie. Her little daughter had been run down by a railroad train and killed. Mary sank into the nearest chair, overwhelmed. What was happening? It was as if the entire family was in the grip of death.

Somehow she went about her duties that day and the day after that. Work was like a soothing balm to heal her melancholy. For the first time, she was almost glad when she received word that she was to go out on another case.

The patient was a woman in her late fifties who was dying of cancer of the stomach. Even Mary, who had little knowledge of the families who made up Pittsburgh's high society, recognized her name. Thirty years ago she had given birth to an illegitimate daughter and refused to give her up. Scandalized, her parents had cast her out of their lives.

From somewhere, Mary had heard that enough money was provided to buy a small brick house in a nearby town along the Ohio. From then on the young woman lived alone with her daughter. It was as if she had been set adrift to float forever on a shoreless sea. She had broken the rules of society and she was doomed to pay the price.

Now in her final days, she lay on her bed in her closet of a room, alone in the world except for her daughter. Only the doctor came and went.

The daughter greeted Mary with little more than a hello. Her face drawn with exhaustion, she moved like a sleep walker as she slowly mounted the stairs to her mother's room. The demands of caring for her mother obviously had taken its toll. Mary did not have to be told that she would be working round the clock in whatever time her patient had left.

During the third night when she was dozing in a chair close by the woman's bedside, the door bell rang. Startled, Mary hurried downstairs and unlatched the door.

A boy dressed in the uniform of the telegraph office held out a buff-colored envelope. "Telegram for Miss Roberts."

"Yes. Thanks." Somewhere she found a nickel for a tip and closed the door.

She stood frozen in the dimly lit entry way, not wanting to open the envelope as she anticipated what might be inside. Like an automaton, her fingers worked open the flap and pulled out the message.

YOUR FATHER DEAD STOP COME HOME IMMEDIATELY STOP UNCLE JOHN

No. Such a thing could not happen. Her father was only forty. He'd never been sick a day in his life. But there were the words, bold and black. Carefully, Mary folded the sheet back in the envelope.

That it was Uncle John who was the person to contact her was so like him. All her life, he had been there to encourage her and help her. He had taught her to ride. He had admired her school work. He was the one she came to with her problems. Dark-haired and slim, he was as handsome as her father.

With the daughter's help, she packed and arranged for a cab to take her to catch the morning train. The winter sky was grey with snow clouds as she climbed into the first coach she came to and chose an empty seat by the window. A discarded newspaper lay on the opposite seat and the headlines caught her eye.

"Tom Roberts shoots self in Buffalo hotel room."

She picked up the newspaper, hardly daring to read the story. What was her father doing in Buffalo? He had said nothing about Buffalo. She looked up, staring at nothing. The door at the end of the car opened and the conductor stepped inside.

When he reached her seat, he asked for her ticket.

"My father. He's committed suicide," she heard herself say.

He glanced at the newspaper in her lap. "Sorry, miss." He waited for a moment. "But I still got to have your ticket."

"Ticket," she repeated stupidly. "Oh, yes." And she fumbled in her purse. "I know I have one." She looked about her seat.

"Look, I need to move along, miss," he said, not gruffly but with a hint of impatience. "But I'll be back."

He had nearly reached the end of the car when she spotted the ticket on the floor between the seats. She picked it up and turned to wave at him. But he must have forgotten about her for he opened the door and disappeared.

The ticket still clutched in her hand, she turned with misted eyes to gaze absently out the window. She and Father had never been close. There were even times when she wasn't sure he loved her. Yet he and Mother had been the center of her life for sixteen years.

She let her head rest against the glass, aware of the train's vibrations, its life. Without thinking, she reached up and drew out her engagement ring hanging on the long ribbon. She wrapped her hand around it, feeling its warmth that had come from lying against her own body.

Since her seventeenth birthday, she had seen dying and death until she had no faith in life. It was as tenuous as a gossamer thread that either the slightest whiff of wind or the most violent of circumstances could sever. One had to be constantly on guard, for the business of living could disappear in an instant.

She opened her fist and glanced down at the modest ring,

tracing a finger over the chips of colored stones and diamonds. Slowly, she felt a certain calm return.

The man who had given her this ring was soon to be her life. He had said his love for her would always be there and she had to believe him. At this moment, she longed to love him in return.

She closed her eyes, weary down to her bones. Weary with death. Weary with trying to heal the misery of the world. Yet she was good at caring for people, at healing. She had an instinct for it and a quick mind that allowed her to keep up with the doctors.

Within a few months, she would graduate. Stanley had promised she could continue nursing after they were married. But what if he changed his mind? Marriage was such a big step in a person's life and she wondered whether it was the right one for her.

Chapter Seven

Mary stood alone in the small office of the church, which for the moment served as her dressing room. In a few moments, she would walk down the aisle on Uncle John's arm to become a man's wife. For most girls, it was a day they had dreamed of all their lives.

But nothing would ever take the place of her pride on graduation day when she had climbed the steps to the stage of the hospital auditorium and received the neatly rolled sheet of parchment tied with a pale blue ribbon. Mother and Stan had clapped, and afterwards at the reception they had offered their congratulations. But she had caught a certain sense of relief in their smiles as if they were glad her days at the hospital were over.

Today would be different. They would beam at her and kiss her. Today was their day to be proud, not hers.

With great care, she lifted the ivory satin dress over her head and settled it in place, hooked up the bodice, and moved to the mirror where she began to arrange her veil.

For a moment, she could only stare. She hardly recognized herself. The young woman in ivory who looked back at her was as elegant, she decided, as any of the brides whose pictures appeared on the society page of the newspaper. Gone was the girl in the crisp uniform with roughened hands, and she felt a sudden rush of fear.

Slowly, she turned away and pulled open the door. Uncle John was waiting for her.

The ceremony and the reception went smoothly and according to plan. But by the time she and Stan reached Bermuda for their honeymoon, Mary's days had become a blur of pain.

Sick with excruciating headaches, she told herself that it was merely a case of exhaustion caused by the months of strain over her father's death. There were days when she could barely raise her head from her pillow. Stan hovered impatiently and she felt miserable about spoiling the trip he had planned with such care. Finally, Stan gave her a shot of morphine and she brightened.

Immediately after they returned from their honeymoon, Stan began to see patients. She was his nurse. In between office hours, she threw herself into the expected housekeeping duties. She baked and cleaned, put up jellies and went to market. There was never a minute in the day to spare and when she climbed up the stairs to bed, she felt a glow of accomplishment.

By Christmas, she knew she was pregnant. From the first, she suffered from nausea and it continued. The days warmed and she grew steadily more miserable. Stanley Junior was born in August. A month later, she went back to helping Stan in the office.

Two years passed before Alan was born. Then came Frederick or Ted as everyone soon called him. After five years of marriage, she and Stan were the parents of three boys whom they adored. But by now her life had become like a crazy balancing act as she tried to care for the children, run the household, and help Stan with the office.

Mary sat by the crib and placed another cool cloth across the forehead of baby Ted, who was recuperating from whooping cough. He had fussed and cried most of the day, and she prayed that soon he would drop off to sleep. Thank heavens that Nell, the hired girl, was feeding the older boys, for it would be hours before Stan returned from evening calls and could help her with the children.

Mary's head throbbed and every muscle ached with longing for sleep. She had not been out of the house for days. She even had trouble recalling what week it was. At first, the terror that little Ted might die gripped them all and she never left his side. Now it was a matter of keeping a watchful eye on the child. Instinctively, she placed her fingers around the baby's tiny wrist. The pulse was stronger and she was relieved.

She glanced around the small room. A single bulb from the wall fixture shed the only light. Heavy curtains were drawn across the window. It was as if she was sitting in a tomb she could not escape. For an instant, she had an insane urge to grab up the baby and race down the stairs and out the door and never come back.

This house was like a prison. Her entire world consisted of its three floors, a demanding husband and three boys, a hired girl who needed supervision, and a noisy dog . . . and always Stan's patients. Visiting hours were between two and four with evening hours from seven until there were no more patients to see. And she had the books to keep. Every fee must be entered and noted when paid.

Sometimes the modest charges were not paid, which came as no surprise, for times were hard. Yet how was she to make the fifty dollars Stan gave her each month stretch to pay the rent, the groceries, a few necessary clothes, and the maid's salary of two dollars a week? There were days when she wondered if the lack of money was to plague her all the days of her life.

Mary lifted the cloth from Ted's tiny head and dropped it in the bowl of water set on the table beside her. He began to cry and she picked him up and sat down in the rocking chair.

Rocking back and forth, the thought of the opera surfaced. For a moment, she savored the vision of the stage and the singers and the costumes and then she stopped, ashamed that she could think of her own pleasures at a time like this. Yet ever since Stan brought home the tickets that one of the senior staff members of the hospital had given him, she had thought of nothing else. It had been so long since she had gone any-where. Surely, little Ted would be well by the magical day.

"Oh, Mrs. Rinehart, it's fit for a queen. And that's the truth," exclaimed Nell as she cautiously touched one of the puffed sleeves of Mary's dress.

Mary stroked the cranberry velvet. Somehow, somewhere Stan had found the money for the material and Mother had made it for her. "It is beautiful, isn't it?" she said.

"You in that dress and Dr. Rinehart in his new top hat. Why, you'll be the finest couple at the opera."

Mary laughed in her happiness. The day had finally arrived. Stan had promised he would be home by seven in plenty of time to change his clothes.

The day flew by. Little Stanley and Alan had taken long naps which gave her time to wash her hair and give her finery one last inspection. Her white gloves didn't look too disreputable. The drop pearl earrings Stan had given her as a wedding pres-ent would be perfect against the dark velvet of her gown.

She eyed the clock in the hallway. Five-thirty. Nell would put the boys to bed so she could dress without rushing. As she started up the stairs, she began to hum the overture of *La Traviata,* already in the mood for the wonderful hours to come.

Seven o'clock came and went. Seven-thirty. Eight o'clock. Six hours later, she sat on the edge of their bed, still in her gown with her hair dressed high on her head, and raised her hand to brush away her tears. The opera was over by now yet she could not bring herself to undress. Behind her on the bed-spread lay Stan's evening suit and elegant silk hat.

Finally, she heard the front door open and then quietly close. Footsteps sounded on the stairs and Stan appeared in the doorway.

"This house was like a prison. Her entire world consisted of its three floors, a demanding husband and three boys, a hired girl who needed supervision, and a noisy dog . . . and always Stan's patients."

"I'm sorry, darling," he said. "It couldn't be helped."

Mary stared at him, speechless for a moment. "What do you mean: 'it couldn't be helped'?"

"I fell asleep on the trolley." He began to undo his tie. "Now let it be, will you?"

She had never lost her temper, never created a scene, but suddenly she began to shout, "Do you know how long I've looked forward to this evening? Do you have any idea what it's like being cooped up with three little boys who can't speak a complete sentence much less carry on a conversation? And you ask me to let it be?"

"Darling—" he implored.

Mary was sick of Stan, sick of always thinking about his needs: making sure dinner was ready the moment he was ready to sit down, ironing his shirts, which she could never get the wrinkles out of, never mentioning how she longed for a new dress because she knew how short the money was. She was sick of it.

"No, I won't let it be." She spun around, grabbed his silk hat and threw it at him. "Here. Take your stupid old hat."

Without a word, Stan reached down and picked up his hat and left the room. She heard him go downstairs and close the door to the office. Undoubtedly, he was going to sleep on the couch that he kept there and she didn't care. If he came back before she calmed down, she might take her dress off and throw it at him, too.

The next morning, she and Stan sat in silence as they picked at their breakfast. Nell poured the coffee and hurried back to the kitchen. Finally, the two older boys appeared and scampered over to their father. He pushed back his chair and scooped them up as he walked toward the hallway. A few moments later, he was out the front door and on his way to the hospital.

Today was Friday. No matter what had happened, there were beds to make and the rooms on the first floor to clean before Stan's office hours. She had bread to bake and the boys to tend to and the mending she had neglected for days. She sighed and went down the hall.

The memory of her burst of temper last night plagued her. Even as Stan had walked down the stairs and disappeared into his office, she had been humiliated at what she had done. In the light of day, she knew perfectly well how hard Stan worked and how good he was with the children.

The prospect of going to the opera had simply overtaken her good sense. Yet what else did she have to look forward to? She longed to feel pride in an accomplishment. She yearned to do something beyond washing diapers, something that required a brain.

That night, Mary met Stan at the door with a cup of coffee as she always did when he came back particularly late from his home visits. He gave her a wan smile as he hung up his coat and hat.

"I'm sorry about last night, darling," he said.

She handed him the coffee and he took a long sip.

"I'm sorry, too."

She followed him down the hall to the kitchen where they usually sat for a few minutes to review the day.

"I couldn't help it. I just fell asleep," he said as he eased onto the straight-backed chair at the far end of the wooden table.

She took the chair next to his. "I don't understand."

"Well, after that appendectomy at the hospital, I got on the trolley to come home and sat down. And the next thing I knew I was almost to Brighton Heights."

"But that's miles past our stop."

"I know."

Stan had not taken a day off since they had returned from their honeymoon, five years ago. There was seldom a day he climbed into bed before midnight. "You should have told me last night," she said, quietly.

His eyes held a smile as he looked at her over the rim of the cup. "There didn't seem to be the right opportunity."

Mary rose and went over to sit on his lap. She wrapped her arms around his neck. "Will you forgive me?"

He kissed her on the lips. "Will you forgive me, is the better question."

The next day Mary sat down at Stan's desk to do this month's billing. She was glad the disappointment of missing the opera was behind her. What good was it to drag around all her resentment about mundane housekeeping and bookkeeping chores when she couldn't do a thing about it?

She was fishing in the drawer for another pad of billing forms when her eyes fell across a faded newspaper clipping. Even without taking it out, she recognized it as her poem that had won a writing contest the Allegheny newspaper had run when she was in high school. The prize had been a dollar.

Rereading it now, Mary was forced to smile at the naiveté of the verse. Yet it wasn't bad. She was reminded of how much she had enjoyed writing it and winning that dollar. She had given the clipping to Stan as a kind of memento when they were engaged but frankly she was surprised he had kept it.

Returning it to the back of the drawer where she had found it, she went on rummaging for the billing forms. Maybe she would write more poetry. Maybe she'd even try her hand at stories.

Stanley junior suddenly ran into the room and yanked at her skirts, and she closed the drawer.

"Mother, come quick."

"Stanley, dear, Mother's busy."

"But Alan's made a mess. He's spilled milk all over. And Puppy's walking around in it."

"Oh, dear." Mary pulled in her breath and prayed for patience as she pushed away from the desk and took his hand. "Well, come on. I'll need to clean it up before Teddy gets into it. Puppy walking around in it is bad enough."

That night after Stan left to make house calls and the boys were in bed, Mary sat down to try another poem. She had to rewrite it several times before she was satisfied, and in the morning she sent it off to the newspaper. A week later, it appeared on the woman's page. She hadn't been paid but it was a thrill to see it in black and white with her name below the title. It was a start.

Next, she tried an article about housekeeping. Certainly, it would have the ring of truth, she thought, for by now it was a subject she knew a good deal about. The *Pittsburgh Gazette* had been seeking articles about practical problems and this one might fit the bill.

Three weeks went by when finally a letter arrived, informing her that the newspaper had accepted her article. A check for twenty-five dollars was enclosed.

"Well now," Stan said when she showed him the check. "This is quite something."

She eyed him and tried to detect what he was thinking. "Isn't it wonderful? Why, if I get busy, I might make enough to buy that coat you need."

He smiled at her and reached out to pat her arm. "I hadn't noticed I needed a new coat."

"Oh, Stan, you know perfectly well you've needed one for years."

"I have a coat. Maybe not the finest looking article of clothing in the world but it will do until we can afford another."

"But that's the point. If I keep selling articles and stories, we'll have a little extra. Oh, I know your practice is growing. But the boys are growing, too, and there always seems to be something that can't be put off. Except your coat. And now you won't have to put it off. You can buy it right now."

He tipped back in his chair and regarded her with amusement. "You're really serious about this little hobby, aren't you?"

She pulled in a breath, hurt at his flippant tone. He was almost laughing at her. To Stan who prided himself on his knowledge of literature, her poem and the article might seem trivial. But they were a beginning. She knew her job was to manage the household and care for the children and she didn't mean to shirk her responsibilities.

To write as she intended to do would take extra time. Yet every night as she tucked the last of the boys in bed, she was totally exhausted. She realized that she had come up squarely against the main question: how great was her resolve?

Chapter Eight

All day as Mary scrubbed floors and cared for the boys, her head filled with ideas for plots. She had decided to try short stories and by the time she sat down at the card table in the sewing room, the stories came together, pouring out faster than her hand could guide the pen across the paper. Once finished, she folded each in an envelope and sent it off to a newspaper or a magazine. To her delight and Stan's astonishment, nearly every story sold.

She kept track of the sales. By the end of the year, she had earned six hundred dollars. But as quickly as the checks arrived, she cashed them, spending the money on clothes for herself and the family, heady with the sense of satisfaction that her work had paid for it all. Though Stan made an occasional cryptic comment about the virtue of saving, she noticed that he did not object to wearing his new coat.

By summer, Stan suggested that they rent a place out of the city.

"It will be cooler and the boys will have space to play."

"But it'll take an hour for you to get home," she said, "and what if you get tied up with a patient and the trains have stopped running?"

He kissed her. "I'll stay in town. A night or two won't kill me."

She and the boys tramped through the woods and went on small excursions along the river. At night, she set up the card table on the porch, ignoring the moths and mosquitos clustered against the screen, to begin her first mystery story.

She already knew the plot. A dead body was found in the lower berth of a train. There was a train wreck. One of the characters was involved in a stock swindle. The story was longer than the others. She decided to call it "The Man in Lower Ten."

That fall, she sold it to *Munsey's* magazine as a serial. She was paid four hundred dollars. The day she received the check, she went to Pittsburgh and bought a large desk to replace her wobbly card table.

The months sped by.

"I think I'll write a play," she announced to Stan one morning as she helped him into his coat.

"Is that so?" He glanced around and grinned at her. "I suppose I shouldn't ask, but what in the world do you know about writing plays?"

Mary opened the door and felt the blast of frigid air. "Not much really. But I'll learn. I already have a good idea for it."

"Well, if I know you, you'll figure something out," Stan replied in that absent manner that told Mary he was already thinking about his day's schedule.

As she went about her household chores that day, her head began to fill with the plot. The characters and their lives that she concocted and then wrote down on paper were her private world. None of it belonged to Stan or the boys or even her mother. There were times when she felt like a stranger in her own family.

By now, she had written forty-eight stories and the words of every one of them had come not out of the head of Dr. Rinehart's wife or even the head of a mother of three boys. They were the product of the imagination and hard work of Mary Rinehart: a person unto herself. She felt like a butterfly who had emerged from its cocoon. She had survived her own bout of diphtheria. She ignored her migraine headaches. Success was something she could touch and hold and spend.

After the sale of "The Man in Lower Ten," she set to work on another mystery. She called it "The Circular Staircase" and section by section, week by week, it also appeared in *Munsey's* magazine.

Six months later, Uncle John came for Sunday dinner. As was his habit, he asked about her latest work.

Finally, he said, "Mary, I think it's time you get a book published."

"I write stories, Uncle John, not books."

"What do you mean? You've written two books that I know of already," he insisted.

"Oh?" Mary laughed.

"I'm talking about those mysteries in *Munsey's*."

"They're just serialized stories."

"They're as long as any book," he persisted.

"I suppose."

"Now listen, Mary. Gather up all the episodes, put them in a box, and send them off to some publisher. My bet is they'll sell in a minute."

That night after Uncle John left and the boys were in bed, Mary went into the sewing room where she did her writing and pulled out the tattered pages of her copy of "The Circular Staircase." She was mildly surprised to note that once straightened and in a neat pile, they added up to more pages than she remembered.

But where to send it? She scanned the titles of the volumes in her bookcase until her gaze settled on a recent novel written by a woman. She pulled it out and found that the publisher was Bobbs-Merrill in Indianapolis.

She knew nothing about the firm. But she knew little about any publishing house. The more she wrote, the more she realized that she had ventured into a field for which she had no training. Her education was limited to high school. She had never gone to college and taken literature classes. It probably was a case of sheer foolishness to think she was able to be anything more than a short story writer.

Yet on her writing table sat a pile of printed pages which Uncle John maintained was a book.

Mary packed up the box containing the collection of episodes of "The Circular Staircase" to Bobbs-Merrill and sent it off. She reminded herself that because it had been a successful serial, the publisher might see it as something the public would like to read in one piece, and her initial doubts softened.

·The day was unusually warm for early May. Armed with a grocery and meat list, Mary dodged around the children in cotton dresses and shirt sleeves playing on the sidewalks as she hurried toward Federal Street. She didn't trust servants to pick out the best meat and vegetables so she continued to do her own marketing. At Kaufman's butcher shop, she pulled open the door and stepped inside.

Kaufman's was a neighborhood institution. Her mother and grandmother and every woman she knew had always bought their meat here. The clean, dry odor of the fresh sawdust scattered across the floor, the carcasses hanging from hooks in the window, Mr. Kaufman in his spotless apron were sights as familiar as her own kitchen.

Mary made her purchases and a clerk began to wrap them when the sharp ring from the store's telephone cut through the babble of customers and Mr. Kaufman moved to answer it.

"Mrs. Rinehart, it is for you," he came over to tell her. "The doctor."

A twinge of panic seized her as she wondered why on earth Stan who was scheduled to be at the hospital should be calling her at Mr. Kaufman's.

"Hello, Stan? Where are you?"

"I'm home. I had to pick up that speech I'm to give this noon."

"Is anything wrong?"

She heard him laugh.

"Not a thing's wrong. I called because I thought you'd want to know that it came."

"What came?"

"The letter from Bobbs-Merrill. Hold on and I'll read it to you." He paused. "It says, 'My dear Mrs. Rinehart: I have read *The Circular Staircase* not only with pleasure but with thrills and shivers'."

"You aren't making this up, are you?" Mary asked.

"Darling, the man wants to buy your book."

As the days moved into summer and the book was about to appear in the bookstores, she wasn't at all sure she had made the right decision. Perhaps she shouldn't have pushed her luck.

Her nagging doubt mushroomed into terror. Every time the telephone rang or she opened the daily newspaper, she was certain she would learn the worst. Perhaps a trip into the quiet of the countryside would soothe her, and she decided to take the boys to stay in a farmhouse friends had told her about that was at least twenty-five miles from Pittsburgh.

They took long walks up deserted roads. They picked blackberries and picnicked along the shores of the nearby lake. But nothing helped. She lay awake all night and snapped at the boys for the slightest misbehavior all day. She had no appetite.

A week later, she realized she had to face whatever criticism might be out there, and she and the boys returned to Pittsburgh. On the front hall table she spied yesterday's edition of the *New York Times*.

Hesitantly, she opened it and turned to the book reviews. At the top of the page in the left-hand column was a review of *The Circular Staircase*. She began to read. After the usual preliminaries, the reviewer discussed her main character, Rachel Innes. He liked her. He thought her convincing, enchanting.

Mary looked up and let out a long breath. The agony of waiting was over and she had passed the test.

The book became an immediate success. The royalties exceeded Mary's wildest dreams. They bought a Premier touring car, hired more servants, and put the boys in private schools.

Instead of renting rooms in a farm house or visiting her aunt, the next summer she and Stan took a cottage on fashionable Bemus Point on the shore of Lake Chautauqua. *The Circular Staircase* had changed their lives.

The house on Beech Street where they had moved last year now overflowed with visitors: an editor from Bobbs-Merrill or her lawyer or a representative from *The Saturday Evening Post* to talk about her next story. The boys seemed to enjoy the change in the pattern of their lives but occasionally Stan grumbled.

"Two nights in a row without half the world sitting down to dinner with us. That's all I ask," he snapped one night as they prepared for bed.

"It's just until I get the rewrite of the play finished."

He eyed her skeptically as he buttoned the top of his pajamas.

"And that's a promise," she added and kissed him lightly on the lips.

A month later, her mother suffered a stroke. Days passed as Mary and Olive sat by her bedside at the hospital, often unsure she would survive the night. Mary put the revisions of her play aside. In time Cornelia Roberts was carried up to the second floor of Mary and Stan's house and settled in the guest room.

Her mother was alive and doctors predicted that her paralysis eventually would lessen. But never again would she knead dough or fix her own hair or walk to the park with her grandchildren.

Mary lay awake at night, filled with the old apprehension about the future that had plagued her ever since her father died. The world she had built over the last four years could disappear in an instant. Her income from writing was over fifty thousand dollars a year now. With a mere twist of fate like a train wreck or a heart attack or arthritis in her hands, she could lose it all.

But once the morning came the demands of every day took

hold. There were the boys to send off to school on time, the meals to go over with the cook, and now her mother to tend to. Mary hired a nurse. Mother seldom complained, but the hurt look in her eyes when Mary left for an appointment or went downstairs to her office to begin the day's writing made her ache with guilt.

Still, the deadlines remained. The new version of the second act of another play and a story for the *Post* were due by the end of the week.

"Stan, do you realize there are writers who would sell their souls to get a story in the *Post*?" Mary said as she climbed into bed one night. "And this year, I've had three accepted."

"Be careful, darling. You might get a swelled head."

Mary laughed and turned off the light. "Not a chance in the world. I don't have time."

Sometimes she felt like a runner, streaking down a steep hill too fast to even see the scene she was passing. But despite the headaches which often plagued her, she always managed to catch her breath and go on. Life never stopped changing, she reasoned. Hers just changed faster than most people's.

But times were also changing for Stan and his health.

"I'll simply have to do something else," he announced one morning as he finished dressing. "No one wants a surgeon whose hands shake."

Mary regarded him with concern. "It's the morphine that does it."

"I know. But without it I can't stand the pain from the arthritis." He brushed his hair in place and reached for his suit-coat. "I suppose I could go back to general practice but these days people want specialists."

"Well, then, that's what you should be."

"But that takes training. And time. Besides, Mary, I'm forty-three years old."

"I hope you're not telling me you're an old dog who can't learn new tricks," she teased.

She waited for his usual humorous comeback but instead Stan faced her with a tired expression. "Tricks are one thing, darling. Practicing in a new field of medicine is something else."

"Surely, you have something in mind," Mary said.

"Pulmonary. There's a great need for better treatment here in Pittsburgh." His voice was suddenly full of enthusiasm.

"That's a wonderful idea. You must go to Vienna to study," Mary added.

"True. But it would mean I'd have to leave you and the boys."

"No, you won't." She smiled. "We'll go with you."

The year in Europe opened up new vistas for Mary. While Stan spent his days at the University and the hospital, she ventured out to deal with shopkeepers and tradesmen. Her halting German gradually improved. She dragged the boys to museums. She found more comfortable living quarters than their hotel. But always she kept on writing. By the end of their stay, she and Stan regularly attended the opera and concerts, and felt thoroughly at home with the variety of languages that swirled around them.

When they returned, Stan was full of plans, full of new confidence, and eager to start up his practice again. He was so busy now that Mary had little trouble convincing him that this was the perfect time to move.

The house of her dreams stood like a grand English country home on a bluff overlooking the Ohio River in the Pittsburgh suburb of Sewickley. It had been built during the Civil War by a railroad magnate and showed its age.

"It'll take a fortune to fix the place up," Stan maintained as they walked around the old house with the bank officials.

"But just look at it. And the ravine back there. It's a perfect spot for the boys to play. Oh, Stan. It's our house. I can feel it."

He laughed. "And I can feel every cent we own disappearing into it like a bottomless pit."

She slipped an arm through his and hugged it close. "But what's money for?"

"I suppose we can call it 'The Bluff.'"

She cocked an eyebrow.

"Don't you see? Here we are about to do everything short of steal to pay for this house. Why, it's a gigantic bluff to even think we can afford it. So why not admit it? We'll call it 'The Bluff.'"

Though Stan was right about having to borrow money to buy the house, Mary was determined. Two months later, they moved in.

Every day, Stan took the train to his office in Pittsburgh and Mary decided that she should also have an office in town. She needed a secretary now and despite the size of the house, there didn't seem a suitable space where the two of them might work.

On weekends, Mary put work aside and concentrated on the boys and social affairs. She found a marvelous cook and the house with its large rooms lent itself well to dinner parties. It seemed impossible that once she had been too timid to ask Stan's superior at the hospital for tea.

Now she thought nothing of inviting the chairman of the symphony board or the wife of the vice president of Carnegie Steel or the producer of her latest play or a U.S. Senator. One of her greatest joys was to sit at one end of the beautiful mahogany dining table set with crystal and fine china and preside over the conversation. She thrived on good talk and her guests provided it.

Her mother regained the use of one hand and took up needlework again. And she seemed to like the companion hired in place of the trained nurse. Mary came by to visit every morning and evening. It wasn't enough time, she knew, but it was all she could spare.

The ache in the back of her neck returned. She wasn't sleeping well. Even in the mornings when she sat down at her desk to begin work, she felt weighed down by the routine of her life. And her thoughts turned to the peace and quiet of the countryside.

In early June, the family packed and headed north to the French River in the Canadian woods. The plan was to stay at least a month. Their accommodations were primitive: tents and meals they cooked themselves out of doors. And gradually, the scent of the pines and the sound of the wind through their towering branches and the icy baths in early morning began to have their soothing effect. The only contact with the outside world was their daily excursion by rowboat to meet the steamer which brought supplies and a newspaper.

On one such morning, Mary sat in the bow with young Stan at the oars. As was her habit, she leaned over and pulled the daily newspaper from the box of provisions, for even in the Canadian woods she could not put the world's news behind her.

"Germans swarm across Belgium." Appalled, Mary read the headline again. There had been talk of war in Europe for months, even years, if all the diplomatic negotiations were counted.

Germany had defeated France forty years ago and seized her richest source of coal and iron. While France seethed, Germany had grown steadily more powerful. Now the Kaiser must have decided that the time had come to expand his country's boundaries once again.

Mary recalled that in June, before she and Stan and the boys had left for the north woods, Archduke Ferdinand, heir to the throne of the Austria-Hungarian Empire had been shot by a Serbian terrorist. Alliances throughout Europe were thrown into turmoil. Thinking about it now, she realized the headlines came as no surprise.

When she handed the newspaper to Stan, he merely glanced at it, scowled, and said nothing.

That night the hoot of an owl was the only sound outside their tent as she and Stan crawled beneath their thick wool blankets and blew out the lamp.

"I've been thinking about the war all day, Stan."

"America will stay neutral," Stan said.

"But did you ever dream Germany would violate Belgium's neutrality? Attacking France is one thing. Marching across Belgium to get to it is another."

"Darling, let's not talk about it. Not now." Stan leaned over and kissed her softly. "We're here for a rest. And to have fun. Now go to sleep."

Mary had been storing up questions to pose to Stan all day and now she was annoyed that he refused to talk about it. She closed her eyes and tried to put the thoughts of the war out of her head. But it was hopeless.

She pictured the lovely Belgium countryside which she and Stan had driven through only three years ago, destroyed by German guns. Didn't the fact that Germany had so openly violated a tiny nation's neutrality signal that this was no ordinary war, if there was such a thing? Germany had bragged for years about its modern army. Was it truly as well trained and invincible as Kaiser Wilhelm always maintained?

An idea seized her. She was wide awake now. She had to go to the war front to see for herself. She reached out and gave Stan's shoulder a firm shake.

"What's wrong?" he mumbled.

"Nothing's wrong. I'm going to the Front."

"That's nice, darling. Now go to sleep."

"You don't understand. I said I've decided to go to the Front."

Stan pushed up on one elbow. "Mary, for heaven's sake. It must be two in the morning."

"What does the time have to do with it?"

"You can't simply make up your mind in the middle of the night to go off to a war that's none of our business."

"Why not?" Mary demanded.

"Because it's idiotic. Now forget it and go to sleep."

But Mary couldn't forget it and a few days later, armed with a growing collection of newspapers, she brought up the matter again.

"Just look," she said to Stan as she held up a front page. "The Belgians are being slaughtered."

Stan continued to pack the box of provisions they were going to take with them on the day's canoe excursion.

"Don't you even care?" she asked, beginning to get annoyed with him.

Stan looked up. "Of course, I care. Obviously, you care. I'm sure lots of people care. But right now you and I and the boys are here in these beautiful woods about to see more beautiful woods. We can't solve Europe's problems."

"I am not suggesting we can solve their problems. I am suggesting that this country needs to know what's going on over there. Really going on. We have no idea what's true and what's propaganda to draw us into the war."

Stan regarded her with impatience. "You are talking utter nonsense."

"I know I'd be a good reporter. Don't you see? This is my chance to prove I can write something besides mysteries."

"Look, darling. There are undoubtedly dozens of reporters over there already. And while you are a wonderful, capable lady, war and women simply don't mix. Now round up the boys and let's get started."

Mary couldn't put the idea aside and that night she wrote a letter to George Lorimer, the editor of *The Saturday Evening Post*. Because he had bought a number of her stories and had praised her work, she was certain he would take her suggestion seriously.

She knew that Lorimer had built the success of the magazine on his unerring instinct for a good story. Though he was known to be personally unsympathetic to America's involvement in foreign affairs, there was a chance he would agree that a woman's view of the Front would sell magazines.

The next morning when they rowed out to the steamship to collect their supplies, she handed the envelope to the captain and asked him to mail it.

When the family returned home, Mary was pleased to find a letter from George Lorimer in which he invited her to come to Philadelphia and explain her idea in more detail.

On a mild September morning, Mary got off the train in Philadelphia and took a cab to the new Curtis Building on Independence Square. In due time, she was ushered into Lorimer's paneled office.

After the usual polite greetings, she decided to get right to the point. "As I said in my letter, Mr. Lorimer, I believe you should send me to the Front."

He sat back in the high backed leather chair and eyed her coolly. With his grey hair cut short against his head, his hawk nose and chiseled features, he reminded her of a Roman tribune. "I've already got two men there."

"You need a woman's point of view."

"Maybe. Maybe not."

"Women make up well over half of your readers."

"True."

He swung around in his chair and stared out the window for several moments before he turned back and demanded, "Do you mean business, Mrs. Rinehart?"

"Do I look like a socialite?"

He lifted an eyebrow. "Now that you mention it, yes."

Mary bridled. "Well, you're wrong. Yes, I mean business. And I can get you the story you want."

"I'll think about it."

"Mr. Lorimer, a war is going on over there. I need to know your answer now."

"What does your husband think of the idea?"

She straightened slightly. "That is a matter between Dr. Rinehart and me."

"Indeed." He drew his long fingers into a tent and studied her for several moments.

"All right. I'll pay your expenses and one thousand dollars for each article. I'll give you some letters of introduction. That may help in London. But from there, you're on your own."

Stan was furious.

"My God, you're thirty-eight," he growled.

"So?" she shot back defiantly.

"And your health is hardly the best."

"Nonsense. My health is fine."

"And what of the boys? Their mother just traipsing off to war as if she were on a holiday—now isn't that something?"

"I'm not going until after Christmas. The boys will be back at school by then. In good hands. We have a fine staff to take care of the house. You are busy with your patients." She smiled at him, determined to keep her composure. "Besides, I'll only be gone six weeks. Eight at the most."

"It's crazy," Stan insisted. "Besides, they'll never let a woman any where near the Front and you know it."

"I don't know any such thing."

For a moment they glared at each other—stubborn in different ways. She refused to allow her decision to make her feel guilty.

"I've already signed the contract."

Chapter Nine

Mary lay awake in her cabin on the main deck of the old *Fraconia* as it steamed toward England. At her feet was the life jacket she had dragged out from its storage space beneath the bunk. The ship had no escort, and beyond masking the portholes and forbidding smoking or lighting of cigarettes on deck at night, there were no precautionary measures against attack from German U-boats.

Out there were the icy waters of the Atlantic. She'd heard that no one could survive that cold for more than ten minutes and the terror of being plunged into the sea was all she could think of.

She turned on her side and bumped against the high wooden side of the narrow bunk. Good Lord, she might as well be in a casket. She opened her eyes and sat up, resigned. There was no hope for sleep tonight.

As she snapped on the overhead light, her eyes fell on the silver framed photograph of Stan and the three boys. She pulled on her dressing gown and got down to study the picture more closely. Those four were the dearest people in the world and with every turn of the engine in the bowels of the ship she was leaving them farther behind.

[77]

Mary sighed. There was no sense going over all that now. She'd made up her mind long ago, last August, that it was important for her to go. The country would be better informed and she'd prove she could write something more than light-hearted mystery stories.

The throb of the engines beneath her bare feet reminded her of the life jacket and she eyed it again. Perhaps if she put it on, she could concentrate on what she had to do in the weeks to come.

Mary reached for the life jacket and put it on. The bulky vest made it impossible to rest her arms by her side and the rough texture of the orange canvas scratched her neck. This was nonsense.

Hadn't she known that from the moment the ship pulled away from the dock danger was to be her constant companion? Going about with a life jacket or its equivalent for the next two months was ridiculous. And so she took it off, stuffed it back into the storage area, snapped off the light, and climbed back into the bunk.

With the morning light, her anxiety eased and after breakfast she sat on the edge of the bunk and opened a small leather-bound notebook. For years, she had taken notes to remind her of events or people or impressions that might be included later in her stories. Sometimes she even recorded her feelings.

But now that was out of the question. For one thing, she had no idea what hands the notebook might fall into. And there was a good chance that eventually it would be released for publication. So what she wrote for the next weeks would be strictly for public consumption. What was truly in her heart, she must keep to herself.

And with fountain pen in hand, she began to write.

January 8, 1915

I was so affected when I got the flowers that I cried. Have the boys and Stan in a folding frame but it hurts to look at them. Everyone says I am doing a remarkable thing but it is not. It is a curious thing that I cannot get insurance. A man can get accident insurance with the amount doubled if there is an accident in the sea. But a woman can hardly get it at all, not at all if she is crossing the ocean. They lay it to hobble skirts. And yet—the talk of women and children first.

That evening at dinner Mary sat next to an eminent English barrister; and immediately social chitchat gave way to a rather candid conversation about the reason for her trip.

"So you see, Mr. Dunston, I really have no permission to go to France," she explained. "I've heard London is full to over-flowing with correspondents who don't have permission either. Perhaps you could suggest someone I might see who would—relent."

He snorted. "I doubt it seriously. For you see, dear lady, there is an excellent reason for your problem. Correspondents are not needed in France."

She eyed him, sipped her wine, and changed the subject. At the moment, there was no point in persisting. The others at the table were also Britishers coming home and undoubtedly the views Mr. Dunston had expressed were for their benefit. She would approach the matter later—when they were alone—and perhaps by then his position would soften.

After that, every time they met on deck or in the salon, she was tempted to bring the subject up again but he eyed her so coldly that she decided not to try. Perhaps it was hopeless.

Then one morning after breakfast, he followed her out on the deck and suggested that when she was in London, she might wish to contact his wife who was Belgian. Mary was delighted and frankly surprised.

She thanked him warmly. How much help this Mrs. Dunston might be remained to be seen. But since it was not always what you knew but whom you knew that counted, she intended to take full advantage of every contact she made.

January 12

Play bridge in evenings, being resolutely cheerful. Captain missed dinner because spent all night on the bridge. He is never off duty these critical days.

January 16

We are nearing the danger zone but everyone is quite calm. Will reach Liverpool next day if all goes well. What is going to happen to me there? I want so much to relieve one of the nurses at the Front for a week or two, but will they take me in?

The train ride from Liverpool to London was uneventful. The *Post* had made reservations for her at the elegant Claridge Hotel and once she was settled, she telephoned Lord Northcliffe, the powerful publisher of the *London Times* to arrange for an appointment. She was well aware that every other correspondent in London had done the same, for it was his lordship who could pull the right strings—if he was so inclined—to get them to the Front.

The next afternoon, dressed in a dark brown suit and appropriately severe hat, and filled with some trepidation, Mary was ushered into his imposing office. In spite of the room's cool temperature, sweat trickled down her sides as she took a chair across the desk from the tall man whom she knew had the power to help her or to prevent her from getting to France.

For a few moments, they carried on the usual polite conversation until finally she drew herself up a little straighter and said as calmly as she could, "Lord Northcliffe, I must get to the Front."

"Absolutely impossible," he said, snapping shut a portfolio that lay on his desk. "Yet—"

He paused, absently fingering his greying mustache as he regarded her. "The truth is we need America."

She waited for him to go on.

"It will take a good deal I suspect to sway her opinion about joining in."

"I'm afraid you're right," Mary agreed. "Which is all the more reason, Lord Northcliffe, that I should be allowed to go to France and report what I see there."

"Perhaps," he mused. "But nevertheless there's nothing I can do."

"Lord Northcliffe, isn't—"

"I am sorry," he cut in, rising and walking around the desk. "Now I'm afraid you must excuse me. I have another appointment."

The abrupt end to the meeting threw her off balance and she struggled for composure. With great effort, she forced a smile as he took her elbow to guide her to the door.

"It has been indeed a pleasure to meet you, Mrs. Rinehart. I do hope that before you return to America, you will join Lady Northcliffe and me for lunch."

She kept the smile pasted on her face. "I'd like that very much. Thank you."

As calmly as if she had not a care in the world, she sailed past his secretary and made her way down the crowded staircase. A stranger seeing her pleasant expression would never guess at the rage she felt inside.

It probably was naive to expect that she could breeze into Northcliffe's office and come away with a promise of a visa, she said to herself. But after he had put her off and implied that now she would meekly head back home, that was too much. Obviously, his lordship did not know a determined woman when he saw one.

January 18

I am a little frightened. Everyone is very kind but I am alone after all. Will I justify the expense of the trip? Will I be able to send any message to the people of America that they have not yet had? But first I have to get there.

January 19

Invited to lunch by Lord and Lady Northcliffe. Because I am a nurse, they tell me that there is a chance to send me on the Belgium Red Cross ship. I can see things first hand at a base hospital.

I am staying on the third floor of the Claridge. An Indian prince and his entourage are the only other occupants of the floor. There are air raids every night and I wonder sometimes how I can find my way back to my room in the dark when I've been out for the evening.

January 20

The most interesting thing about this morning is that I lived to see it. The attack around Yarmouth not seventy miles away was too close for comfort. Five people killed.

By mid-day on the twenty-first, Mary again met with Lord Northcliffe at his office. At their meeting over luncheon two days before, he had suggested that she go on the hospital ship. She had to admit that her past nursing experience gave the idea merit. Once when she'd talked to Stan about her going, she had suggested as much herself. But nursing was not—nor in truth had it ever been—what she intended to do in France. She would go as a full-fledged correspondent. Period. But there was no need to say as much to Lord Northcliffe.

"You understand, Mrs. Rinehart, that I still have grave doubts as to whether you will reach France. But just in case, I have jotted down a few suggestions of where you should go and whom you should see." And he handed her two sheets of paper.

Mary began to put them in her purse.

"No, no. Read them," he insisted.

"Right now?"

"Of course."

His intensity touched her. She glanced down at the pages and began to read.

"Get Dr. DePage to provide auto and military pass to take you to Dunkirk.

"At Dunkirk, go to Hotel des Arcades and ask for Mr. Singleton.

"Ask to be presented to King and Queen of Belgium at La Panne.

"Keep all your trunks locked."

The list went on. Finally, she looked up to meet Northcliffe's gaze.

"How can I thank you?" she asked, quite taken aback by his kindness.

"You have to get there before any thanks are due," he said gruffly. "But in the remote possibility that you do, keep your eyes open and write what you see. That's all the thanks I require."

Mary carefully placed the list in her purse, they exchanged good-byes and she left. Outside, the grey skies had turned to rain. For a moment, Mary stood in the shelter of the doorway looking up the street for a cab when she decided instead to walk for awhile. As she strode along the sidewalk crowded with uniformed men, dodging the puddles and raised umbrellas, she felt the soft rain against her face wash away the edges of her anxiety.

She had convinced Lord Northcliffe of the seriousness of her mission. But that was not enough. What she must have was a visa and somehow she had to find a way to get it.

Chapter Ten

That evening promptly at 6:30, Mary rapped on the door of a room on the mezzanine of the Savoy Hotel. Thanks to Mrs. Dunston, she was about to meet with the officials of the Belgian Red Cross.

Three years ago in this very hotel she had swept down the red-carpeted grand staircase, her hand on Stan's arm, on their way to the theater. Thinking about that carefree night, it seemed like make-believe. Never would she have dreamed then that she would be here now trying to go where she might very well be killed.

When the door opened, she was ushered into a small dark room thick with cigarette smoke. Three men were grouped in one corner. A huge white-haired man with a trim beard who wore a military-style cape sat at a desk. When he noticed her, he rose, bowed, and introduced himself in French as Dr. DePage. Mrs. Dunston had explained that he was the physician to the Queen of the Belgians and head of the Belgian Red Cross.

Beside him was a man who was apparently a kind of secretary. He was nearly a head shorter than Dr. DePage and fifty pounds lighter. His quick smile and kind eyes eased some of her apprehension. As he drew up a chair for her, he introduced himself as Mr. LeClerq and explained that he was to serve as the interpreter.

She carried a letter from Lord Northcliffe suggesting that she be allowed to go over on the hospital ship. She knew full well that it was more acceptable for her as a former nurse to remain among other women in the relative safety of hospitals. But she was determined to tell her story from a larger view. She would use Northcliffe's letter only as a last resort.

"Dr. DePage, the plight of the Belgian people is well known now. But the American people know nothing of the conditions faced by the Belgian army."

She kept her eyes on the huge man as her words were translated but his face was a mask. She continued.

"Sir, I know your principal concern is with the hospitals. But the Red Cross deals with far more. Let me see it and tell about it. Let me see the refugees behind the Front. Let me see the wounded. The Belgians who have been mutilated. So that I may tell America."

Mr. LeClerq translated. Dr. DePage responded. "It is true what you say. The Americans may know of the ravaged land-scape but nothing of the rest." He studied her for a moment before he went on.

"The plight of the army is very grave, Madame. It is cut off from supplies. It is ill-equipped. Even the water is bad. And the conditions in the trenches are unspeakable: frozen feet, gangrene, typhoid. Our gallant men are holding on—desper-ately—until the Allies can help."

Mr. LeClerq's matter-of-fact translation failed to hide the doc-tor's deep feelings.

"The nursing care, the hospitals are almost nonexistent at the Front. Bandages are washed in the streams. The wounded lie on cold stone floors for hours as they wait for care." He shook his head sadly. "Madame, this is no place for a woman."

Mary leaned forward, her hands clutching her purse. "Dr. DePage, *The Saturday Evening Post* sent me here because they believe I have the ability to report the true story. Please let me see it and I pledge to you that I will tell what I see."

[86]

When the secretary finished the translation, the doctor signaled to the men who stood in the shadows. They conferred in quiet tones. Mary held her breath. She felt like a patient in an operating room as the doctors decided her fate.

Finally, Dr. DePage turned to face her.

"We have decided, Madame Rinehart, that you must tell our story. You will have the necessary papers. Permission to stay as long as you must. And we will, of course, provide you with proper escort."

Mary blinked back the tears of her gratitude to this man who had listened. She thanked him profusely. Mr. LeClerq escorted her to the door and told her he would be in touch with her tomorrow with all the details.

January 21

I am to go to the firing line. No woman has gone there yet. They want me to see everything to tell the *Post*'s readers. They are anxious that I influence public opinion on their behalf.

I am to go to Calais on Tuesday escorted by the secretary's brother who also speaks English. Dr. DePage will meet me there and I shall have an auto at my command during entire stay. Can take a suitcase with me. I demanded a photographer but they reluctantly refused.

This afternoon I went to the Belgian legation to get my passport visa. A difficulty has arisen. The result of arbitrary orders from Calais to allow no one to land. But on going to Lord Northcliffe, he waved it aside.

"You will go," he said. "That's all. You'll go."

I am to have the French legation visa, my passport, and the pink slip of the Belgian Red Cross. It seems I have the fourth one ever issued which tells me that of all my official papers, it may serve me the best after all.

Sidney MacDonald, our dear friend from Vienna days, has inoculated me against typhoid, a thousand needles in the left arm. It is already beginning to swell and ache.

January 22

Been wretched all day from inoculation. Arm swollen and joints very painful. Went to Selfridge's late and bought rain cape, a dressing gown that will be warm and take little space, and a plain black silk dress, the latter in case I see the Queen of Belgium.

A telegram says General Melis head of Belgium forces will meet me at Calais. Northcliffe is sending a man named Steadman with me as well as my "secretary" Mr. Lazard. I cannot take a camera but they will take pictures for me over there.

A wretched day, foggy, gray with snow this morning that has turned to rain. A good night for the airship raid.

January 24

Went to the service at St. Paul's. It was frightfully cold and dark. The body of the church filled with troops. Boys. I could hardly see my prayer book for tears.

I can write nothing more in this little book for a time. It goes sealed to Sidney MacDonald. The only thing I fear about this trip is pneumonia or influenza. But in the remote contingency of my not returning in four weeks, he will send it on to Stan.

For a few days then—

At London's Victoria Station, Mary was searched by a woman from Scotland Yard. With maddening thoroughness, she inspected Mary's Red Cross card and her visas. Finally, the inspector let her through.

The station was choked with troops and their families. The cavernous space was curiously quiet, like a church, with men

LA GUERRE EUROPÉENNE DE 1914-1915

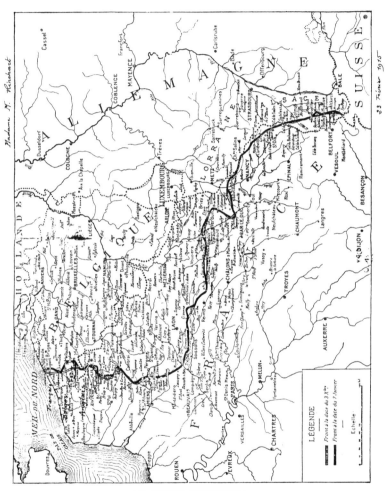

LE FRONT OCCIDENTAL

Mary's map of the Front, dated February 23, 1915.

and women barely speaking, standing apart as if to touch would shatter their sturdy resolve to see through the agony of leave-taking.

Mary wore a new dress of black taffeta, which rustled outrageously, a fur wrap, and a corsage of red roses. At the hotel, she had imagined the festive clothes might take the edge off the good case of nerves she had developed, and when the management had presented her with the corsage she had pinned it on without thinking. Now she felt miserably out of place and embarrassed as she made her way through the crowd of olive drab.

The train rolled slowly out of the station. The passengers around her were soldiers alone in their thoughts as they stared out the windows. She sat back against the seat, trying not to think about the barriers that still might prevent her from boarding the ship at Folkestone.

Last night, she had mailed her first notebook to Sidney MacDonald for safekeeping. And just before turning off the light, she had written a letter to each of the boys. Lighthearted letters that talked of the weather and asked about Jock their dog and how they were doing in school. To Stan, she had written of their lovely Christmas together. Now she wondered what the men around her had said to their loved ones.

The pier was jammed with men and equipment. Small boats and ones large enough to be considered ships were lined up alongside. Mary struggled through the crowd, realizing for the first time that she had not the slightest idea which of the vessels was going to Calais. She peered around her in the half darkness to catch sight of anyone who might be in charge.

An officer passed her and she swung around and tapped his shoulder. "Pardon me—" she began, but he continued on his way.

She pushed on, past grim-faced men too occupied to even notice her. Finally, she spied a naval officer who was directing a stream of soldiers onto a small ship painted a conspicuous white.

"Excuse me, but is this the boat that's to go to Calais to-night?" she shouted through the din.

He gave her a distracted nod.

"Finally. I thought I'd never find the right one," she said, taking out her visas as she started to walk past him up the plank.

But she had gone only a few feet when his hand gripped her arm and pulled her backwards. "No civilians. Sorry."

She shrugged loose. "I demand to see the captain."

"Madam—"

"You don't understand, Lieutenant. I have permission. See here." She thrust her visas in his face again. "No matter what you say, I am coming aboard."

Before he could catch her, she broke loose of his hold and pushed past him up the plank, her suitcase clutched in her arms, and into the mass of soldiers gathered on the deck. She would kick and scream before she would let anyone try to take her off.

But apparently the naval officer forgot about her. Or perhaps he had decided he would leave her to the captain. Minutes went by and no one came after her. The engines started and the lines were cast off. Mary took a deep breath in relief and tried to find some place to sit down.

They were well out of the bay before Mary went up to the bridge in search of the captain who accepted her presence without a word of objection. When he realized that she was the only woman on board, he arranged for a piece of canvas to be stretched out from the bridge for shelter against the raw January wind.

The boat went at top speed, her lifeboats slung over the sides and ready for lowering. The threat of attack by German U-boats was always present. Though lookouts were posted on all sides of the boat, it seemed to Mary that they watched everything but the water. She was terrified, certain that every piece of floating debris was a submarine's periscope, and she could not take her eyes off the water.

In a casual conversation with the captain, she learned that

their destination was not Calais as she had thought but Boulogne.

"But my visas and permits are for Calais," she told him.

"It can't be helped, Madam. Those are my orders."

She had visions of growing old waiting for new permission to go to Calais. And of going by foot. She thought of the correspondents in French jails. But worrying about it now solved nothing; and she drew her fur close around her, buried her face in its collar, and kept her eyes on the dark water.

By the time the boat docked and she struggled with suitcase in hand down the narrow gangplank, her resolution had returned. And as she strode up the quay along the rain-slick cobblestones, she barely felt the chill of the damp air.

Her ploy was to assume an air of authority when she confronted the customs officials. And it seemed to work, for aside from a few questions, she sailed right through. In less than an hour she headed toward the station and the ticket window. As if there was no question about whether she had the right to buy one, she demanded a first class ticket to Calais. The agent hardly glanced at her as he took her money and shoved the ticket beneath the wrought iron barrier.

Now it was a matter of waiting for whatever train was going in that direction. As she glanced about, she began to feel immensely pleased with how far a little bravado had brought her in such a short time.

A tremendous craving for a cup of hot coffee suddenly came over her and she looked around for a cafe of some sort. She began to make her way through the crowd when suddenly along the track ahead appeared a makeshift hospital train. It was British and, from under the flickering arc lights, she could see a nurse step out of one of the cars. Then with the care that comes with pain, a man slid out along a plank placed through the window, pushing himself with his hands, his two bandaged feet held in the air.

"Frozen feet from the trenches," said someone standing next to her.

The man was lifted down and placed on a truck. Immediately, another man took his place. In turn, another man took his place and so it went, endlessly it seemed.

The next car was unloaded. Mary could make out an iron framework on which stretchers, three high, were suspended inside. Through an open window in the center of the car, stretchers were handed over the sill, one by one, to the orderlies outside. Each stretcher was laid gently on the platform in the icy cold wind. Not a man uttered a sound. For a few moments, Mary stared at the line of stretchers and then her attention returned to the hospital train.

A tall officer, probably not more than twenty, was taking the stretchers as they were handed out the car windows, assuming the greatest weight. With marvelous gentleness, he lowered them onto the platform. He had a trick of the wrist that enabled him to reach up, take hold, and lower the stretcher without freeing his hands.

The wounded did not speak or move. It was as if they were beyond their limit of endurance. The line grew and grew.

Slowly, Mary turned away, her feeling of elation replaced by the horror of what she had seen. She had worked in a charity hospital and had seen the worst. Or so she had thought until tonight.

Calais was a mere twenty miles north but the trip in the crowded, filthy train took three hours. Exhausted, Mary finally staggered out of the station and lugged her suitcase through the dark streets. Twice she lost her way before she reached the ancient hotel where General Melis was to meet her in the morning.

Her room was like a great tomb lighted by the single candle the concierge had supplied. The paper was peeling from the walls. The dank air smelled of mold; the water in the pitcher on the bedside table was frozen. Mary eyed the bed uncertainly but her weariness left her no choice. She unbuttoned her shoes and took them off. And then, fully clothed, she eased down on the lumpy mattress and almost instantly fell asleep.

According to plan, an aide to General Melis picked her up late the next morning. In an open grey car with "Belgian Red Cross" on each side of it, they headed northeast in a bitter wind. The landscape was an expanse of flat fields and canals and roads bordered by endless rows of trees bent forward like marching men.

At first there were few signs of war, only an occasional grey lorry laden with supplies for the Front and great ambulances with a red cross on top as a warning to airplanes. But gradually earthworks that held the trenches began to appear. By fading daylight, the landscape was desolate and warlike.

In the half dark, the car finally entered La Panne. It was a scraggly little town with a single street and a row of villas built on the sand dunes overlooking the sea. The few trees clung to the dunes, twisted in the channel winds. Slowly, the car pulled into the courtyard of what six months ago had been a fashionable seaside resort hotel. In place of carriages or automobiles the space was crowded with ambulances.

Mary got out stiffly. After fifty miles in bitter cold in an open car, she was chilled to the bone but still eager to see everything. She looked up at the pleasant building which such a brief time ago had been a place people came for holidays, and she realized that the windows had been painted white with a red cross in the center of each.

The large central door opened and an older man in uniform appeared, Dr. DePage. They shook hands, and he ushered her inside.

"This is the first hospital behind the trenches," Dr. DePage explained. "The hospital of the Queen."

Mary nodded, hearing the almost reverential tone as Dr. DePage spoke of the Queen of the Belgians. What kind of woman could inspire such feelings? Mary had asked permission to interview the King and she wondered if he commanded the same respect.

A nurse emerged from a hallway and spoke to the doctor for a moment. With a tired smile, she introduced herself to Mary and indicated she should follow her. Quickly, she led the way up to a small attic room until recently probably a servant's room. Tonight it would be hers.

"There will be dinner later, Madame," the nurse said quietly. "But first Dr. DePage wishes that you see the hospital."

Downstairs, Mary and Dr. DePage walked carefully along the narrow space between the rows of wounded who lined the corridors. Occasionally, he stooped to say something to one of the men—or rather one of the boys, for that's what most of them were. Always the response was a grateful smile.

The card room was now a chapel. The parlors were filled with the bandaged convalescents, blind or so horribly maimed that she felt the bile rise in her mouth at the sight of them.

Trained as a nurse, Mary had seen typhoid and dysentery cases at their worst, men literally torn apart by machinery in the mills, women with their insides eaten by the lye they had swallowed. But none of it compared with the carnage and human wreckage she saw now.

The tall doctor led the way to the kitchen where their dinner was being prepared. She was numb with fatigue and knew she should eat. But the misery around her had stifled her appetite. What was the good of it, these men and boys maimed or dying? Was it to maintain old men's dreams of glory or simply to preserve a boundary line, a few meters of land?

As tactfully as she could, she excused herself and climbed the stairs to the little room. She would record the day but there was no way she could write of the pain in her heart.

January 27

Two weeks and four days since I left New York and here I am laying out my cold cream and my toothbrush as calmly as though German guns were not banging away, destroying Nieuwpoort four miles away. I can even see them flash now and then.

I am at La Panne, a small sized seaside village, twenty miles from Dunkirk and only three miles from Furnes which the French and Belgians have just evacuated. The shelling had ceased when we came through but the town was dead, literally empty and largely destroyed. As the only way out of La Panne is by road, if the Germans get that, it is good bye for sure.

Mary closed the small reporter's notebook and tucked it back into her suitcase. She took off her dressing gown, blew out the candle, and wearily climbed under the blankets on the narrow bed. As she lay in the darkness, she became aware of the sounds: the guns pounding in the distance, the moans and the shrieks of the wounded below. In the next room, a man—delirious with pain—was singing "Tipperary."

My dear God, what is the use of this dreadful war?

January 28

11 p.m. Dunkirk.

I have passed through my first bombardment by aeroplanes. A frightening experience surely. And now we are in darkness for word has come that a zeppelin is on the way. Air ships are bad enough but the zeppelin fearful. It is probably true for I hear firing now.

In this great vault of a room, I have only one candle. The heavy curtains are pinned together. Some of the people are already in the cellar but Mr. Singleton who has been assigned as my escort thinks it foolish. So I am here. This is France now. Not Belgium. At La Panne so many spoke English.

More firing. It must be close. A wonderful moonlight night.

Came from La Panne this afternoon at a furious rate—almost upsetting—in General Melis' closed limousine.

Hardly an inch of road not filled with cannon transport wagons and Paris buses now painted dull gray and full of French soldiers.

There is a difference in morale of French troops and Belgians. Hard to define but there.

Chapter Eleven

Mary pulled on her sturdy boots, put on Stan's soft-brimmed hat she had brought along, and slung her rain cape over one arm. This morning General Melis was to take her to Ypres to see what was left of the five-hundred-year-old city after the German bombardment.

For days now she had trudged behind the general, trying valiantly to keep up with his long strides, her boots soaked within minutes, her bones chilled by mid-day. She returned exhausted each night to crawl between the clammy sheets of her lumpy bed. But none of it compared with what the soldiers went through and she never dreamed of complaining.

This morning as she hurried downstairs, she smelled the rich aroma of coffee and realized how good a cup or two would taste before the journey ahead. As she walked toward the dining room, she passed the corner where she and three Russian grand dukes had sat out last night's raid. Others had gone to the cellar but when the dukes continued to calmly sip their demi-tasses, Mary had decided she would, too. Together they had groped their way out of the darkened dining room and found a safe corner to sit.

Mary suddenly heard someone call out "good morning" and she turned to see Captain Singleton, who had been assigned as her escort, coming toward her. "I understand you refused to go to the cellar last night."

"Oh, I was perfectly safe, Captain. The grand dukes and I were sitting over there." As she pointed to the corner, she noticed for the first time that above the spot was a glass skylight. That they had escaped from a piece of shrapnel shattering the window was pure luck. And she burst out laughing.

"Sorry?" apologized the slender captain, not understanding the joke.

She caught her breath. "I'm not even sure it's funny. But look at the ceiling over the corner where we sat. It's a skylight."

Captain Singleton stared first at the glass ceiling and back at Mary.

"A roof of glass was our protection." She began to laugh again. "And there we were, sipping coffee, oblivious, as innocent as babes."

Later as Mary climbed into the general's limousine, she was grateful for that earlier moment of humor. In the distance, she heard the sound of shelling. The automobile crept along the Dunkirk streets pockmarked with craters and littered with rubble. They neared the drawbridge in the town's wall and stopped before the guards.

Mary handed one of the men her Red Cross slip. He studied it for a moment, then looked at her suspiciously. For the first time, it occurred to her that her name was of German origin. Perhaps he thought she was a spy. The soldier turned to talk to an officer. Mary pictured herself being dragged from the car and thrown into a damp cell. The two men continued to mumble gravely, occasionally eyeing her. Finally, with a shrug, the officer nodded, and the car was allowed to go through.

The guns boomed in the distance and they inched along the highway until they reached Ypres. Entire blocks had been transformed into huge piles of rubble. Here and there, a lonely church spire rose from the midst of the debris. There was no sign of life. The driver steered the car along the crater-filled streets. Finally, he braked to a stop and she and the general got out. Immediately, several officers appeared. As salutes were given and introductions were made, she felt the men's stares.

"You must excuse them, Madame," said General Melis. "You are the first woman who is a foreigner to view all this. The great Cloth Hall. And the Cathedral. Five hundred years old. Gone." He slowly shook his head.

Mary shivered, the sound of shelling at the edge of her consciousness as she looked around her, taking mental notes of the wanton destruction, the obliteration of a city. Around her were the skeletons of what had been a neighborhood. Only one house remained intact. She picked her way across the street and examined it more closely. As she peered through the door, she realized there was no house at all; only the front wall stood like part of a ghostly stage set. And behind the wall amid the destruction of the rest of the house stood a brass bed, fully made.

She stared, transfixed, until she felt a gentle touch on her shoulder.

"Madame Rinehart?"

She turned and looked up into the bluest eyes she had ever seen.

"May I present, Monsieur le Commandant Delaunois," she heard General Melis say.

No more than thirty years old, Delaunois was nearly six feet tall and trim. He wore the officer's belted tunic and high boots. His hair was fair. He gave a slight bow.

"May I say how pleased we are that you are here, Madame?"

She shook his hand. Unlike most other Belgians she had met, his English was impeccable.

The shells began to come closer.

"Please, we must seek shelter," he said, as he took her elbow to guide her toward a cellar. Awkwardly, she made her way down the steep stone steps, out of the bright morning light, into the darkness lit by a single candle. He took her to a corner and indicated she should sit down. The floor was of damp earth. General Melis sat beside her. The driver of the car and an aide stood nearby, their backs against the stone foundation.

The shelling was close now and for a few moments no one spoke. She wondered how long a person's nerves could survive the possibility of imminent death that hung over them in this cellar.

Suddenly, she smelled the sulfur of a match struck and saw the glow of a cigarette. From behind it came the voice of the commandant, "The worst is for the children."

The general must have told the commandant she had come to learn the facts. His words held a detached quality as if he were making a report to superiors. And yet as he stood next to her in the dim light, she sensed—just below the surface—the agony he felt over what he saw and experienced every day, but never dared to reveal.

"Yes," he continued. "Like the little girl we saw yesterday. She was sitting by the side of the road with her sister. The blood had dried over the wounds. But it was not until she held up her arms that I saw them." He took a long drag on his cigarette. "From the look of the wounds, her hands had been cut off by a sword. Of course, only the officers carry swords," he explained quietly, matter-of-factly.

Mary held her breath as she listened.

"The child looked up as we drove past. 'Monsieur', she called. 'Can you tell me when my hands will grow back?'"

Mary stared at the shadowy face of the commandant, unable to respond to the horror he had described. If she wrote about it, how would an American who had seen none of this misery ever believe that a German officer had cut off a child's hands? There were millions of Germans in the United States—good American citizens—who would deny such an atrocity was possible. Yet the commandant had seen it with his own eyes.

"But then the old people suffer, too." He dropped the cigarette and methodically crushed it out with the heel of his boot. "We found an ancient peasant not far from here tied to a hitching post. I could not believe that he was still alive.

"Riding with the general, she'd seen the men coming back from the trenches. . . . some bandaged, the white gauze strangely iridescent in the moonlight."

As we laid him out upon the ground to try to give some aid, we counted eighty-four bayonet holes on his body."

General Melis said, "You understand now, Madame Rinehart, the atrocities which some say are imagined are, in fact, quite real."

She nodded.

"But come. The shelling has stopped for awhile and we want you to see No Man's Land."

At last she was to go. For weeks, she had heard gruesome tales of life along the Western Front in the network of trenches, which stretched for six hundred miles across France and Belgium. On command, infantrymen with fixed bayonets, facing a barrage of artillery and machine gun fire, climbed out of the trenches through entanglements of barbed wire toward the enemy. In some places, only a few hundred yards of treeless ground separated the opposing lines. No Man's Land, it was called.

She knew that to tell the true story of this war and its unspeakable horrors, she must see as much as she possibly could. First-hand. Now she was to have the chance.

Riding with the general, she'd seen the men coming back from the trenches for two days rest and the ones going up again. They moved past the car she was in—some bandaged, the white gauze strangely iridescent in the moonlight. Here and there, as they passed, a man blew on his fingers for the wind was bitterly cold.

She did not have to see the men, for she could smell them. By now they were numb to it but the stench that came from moldy clothes, urine and feces floating in the stagnant water, and decaying bodies was a smell she was certain she would never forget.

As they moved along the side of the road past the car, they were entirely silent. Even their boots made no noise. They loomed up like black shadows and then were gone, swallowed by the night.

This afternoon Mary and General Melis drove for perhaps an hour. The roads clogged with men and transport wagons made the going slow. Finally, the general's car drew up to a partly destroyed building and she noted that another limousine was parked nearby.

"The briefing will be here and then—"

"General Melis, this other automobile—"

"Ah, yes. The other members of the press."

Mary's heart sank. "I see."

"But, Madame, you are the only woman." His usual serious expression was softened by the kindness in his eyes. But she didn't need his sympathy.

She drew herself a little straighter. She had managed through guile and intelligence to get the proper visas that no other correspondent was able to obtain. She had sometimes risked her life to see and talk to the men on the Front. Yet now the same reporters who had spent their days in the safety of London were given free access to No Man's Land.

But there was nothing to be done about it. And as cooly as she could, she said, "I'm sure it makes no difference."

He nodded solemnly. "Of course."

The presence of the reporters infuriated her. This was supposed to be her show. But purposefully, she greeted the half dozen reporters in a friendly, offhand manner. The two Americans and Britisher from the *London Times* whom she knew responded politely enough. When the briefing about the German position was over, they were escorted outside to go several miles down the road where the third Belgian army was headquartered. There they would be at the edge of the trenches.

She strode along with General Melis by her side. Her initial annoyance at finding the other reporters here had waned. The general was quite right. She was the only woman among them. Further, she had permits for an indefinite stay while the men could stay for only twenty-four hours. What truly mattered was that she finally was to go into No Man's Land.

The night was filled with a fierce wind and driving rain. It was nearly midnight when they reached the trenches and started slowly through the wire. To her chagrin, her rain cape caught on the barbed wire and it took several minutes before it was freed. The German trenches were only a thousand feet beyond.

Their objective was a ruined church tower, four hundred feet out in the flooded plain on a rise of ground and only six hundred feet from the German parapet. There a Capuchin monk wearing a soldier's uniform stood guard as an observer.

The only means of reaching the tower was along a narrow and mud-slick dike. No tree, no shrubbery, no house gave any shelter. General Melis had warned their small group that if the moon came out they could be seen. If they moved, they would be shot.

Worse than the moonlight would be a fusée—those magnesium flares which the British called starlights. Whatever one chose to call them, they were like a white rocket bursting silently overhead, their unearthly brilliance lighting up everything below.

By now Mary and the others had come to the end of the trenches. The plan was to go out along the dike one by one. She hung back, watching as each man started out. There was a strange, horribly surrealistic quality about the scene. And then it was her turn. Her finger tips were numbed with fear and she was barely able to breathe. Every sense was as sharp as a finely honed razor. Sound seemed unnaturally loud. The smells were nearly unbearable. As she stood there, hesitating, she suddenly had a terrible urge to urinate.

"Madame, you need not come along," whispered the officer beside her.

Mary looked out at the shadowy water and breathed the stench of the bodies that lay there, decaying in death. It could have been the channel Styx. The narrow path across it looked endless. What if she was shot up there? Would she fall into the water and drown like so many men had done?

"Madame—"

"Please, sir. I am here to see. And I intend to do so." Saying the words restored her courage; and gathering her cape around her, she started out.

The moon had slipped from behind the film of clouds and she could see the German parapet a few hundred feet away. For an instant, she nearly froze in her terror. A German sniper might raise his rifle at any instant and find an easy target. But she went on until, finally, she reached the ruined church.

Two sides of the steeple were still standing and the priest had a rope ladder to reach the top. In the rubbish at the base he had cleared a space for the graves where he had buried the men who had fallen. Suddenly, she felt something soft rub against her ankle and she looked down to see a cat, which she presumed belonged to the priest.

She leaned down to stroke the animal's fur as she listened to the priest explain his duties and to the officer's translation. The moon was so bright that she could see the very sandbags that formed the German parapet. Down the line, rifle firing had started again and a battery thundered constantly. The reality of the war was all about her and yet for an instant, she felt as if she was looking at a moving picture.

Whispered questions from the priest's visitors and his quiet answers went on until it was time for the return trip. The officer led the way with Mary just behind him, holding her breath again. They moved quickly and she concentrated to keep her footing. The journey back seemed even longer and she felt the pain of a blister rubbed raw where one of her heavy boots chafed her heel. She began to limp. But to slow down might mean death.

Eventually, they reached the trenches again. The terror inside her gradually subsided; and by the time she climbed back into the general's car, a certain sense of triumph began to emerge. After all, she had gone to No Man's Land, a feat no other woman had accomplished. And she had come back alive. Most important, she would be able to tell the tale.

In fact, the chances were good she would go again. But even if she went out every three days as the soldiers did, she knew she would never grow used to the stark terror or the ugliness or mockery of killing men for what reason no one yet could explain.

Chapter Twelve

The touring car raced along the pitted roads choked with men and machines as the night faded into day. Mary was gripped with a stabbing headache and chills and suspected she was on the verge of the flu. But under the circumstances, never would she say a word to anyone about how miserable she felt. Once back at the hotel, she found a cup of coffee and a piece of crusty bread for her breakfast, mounted the stairs, and crawled into bed.

That night, dreams of men with eyes hollowed in exhaustion and arms blown off filled her troubled sleep until finally she gave up, reached for her dressing gown, and attempted to gather herself together for the day ahead.

A knock sounded at the door and she went over to open it. To her chagrin, she stood facing a Belgian officer, mustached and in proper uniform. Quickly, she drew her dressing gown closer around her.

"Madame Rinehart?"

"Yes."

"A message for you, madame," he said in French and handed Mary a long envelope. With a click of his heels, he gave a small bow and left.

Mary stared after him for a moment before she stepped back into the room and closed the door. She saw now that the envelope was closed with an official-looking seal. Intrigued, she opened it and drew out a sheet of heavy paper bearing the royal crest. The message was in French.

> Madame Rinehart, His royal majesty King Albert of the Belgians will see you at three o'clock tomorrow at his villa in La Panne.

It was signed by the king's secretary, Mr. Ingelbleek.

Astounded and delighted, Mary reread the words. She had hoped for an interview but because she had never received any response to her requests, she had presumed they had been refused.

February 4

> I'm very nervous. And I have nothing suitable to wear but there is no help for it, I guess. At the least, I must have my hair washed and find a pair of fresh white gloves.

The next day was grey and cold but fortunately the touring car was enclosed, and considering the tremendous speed at which they were traveling, Mary was reasonably comfortable as she sat next to Captain Singleton, who had been assigned the duty of accompanying her to the modest villa occupied by the royal family.

She had made up a list of questions for the interview and felt reasonably at ease about her meeting with King Albert until she was greeted by his secretary who began to instruct her on her deportment. She was to stand no closer than six feet from his Highness. She was not to speak unless he spoke first. By the time she was ushered into the room where the meeting was to take place, she was nearly rigid with fear over making some monstrous error of protocol.

The drawing room was large and the flowered chintz that

covered the furniture gave it an informal air like that of a seaside home where a family spent its holidays. A fire burned in the fireplace. At one end of the marble mantel was a teak cigar box. Two tables littered with papers were placed nearby. The windows overlooked the sea.

Suddenly, a door opened and a tall man entered. He wore a blue uniform but without the usual high boots or puttees. His hair was blond and his eyes an intense blue. Mary's first impression was that King Albert was much younger than she had expected, perhaps no more than his mid-twenties.

She smiled and he regarded her politely but did not speak. Several minutes went by but the king said nothing. Desperately, she recalled the instructions that she was to say nothing until spoken to. Still, the awkward silence was growing intolerable.

Mary gave him a small smile. "You know, sire, you are supposed to speak first."

The King's eyes widened slightly. "I am?"

She nodded. "Yes, sire."

He smiled. "Well, then suppose we sit down," he suggested and pulled a chair out for her.

But the problem did not disappear, for protocol dictated that she must not take a seat before the king. She looked from the offered chair to King Albert. "Sire—" she began.

"Please, Madame Rinehart," he said, smiling slightly now as he anticipated what she was about to explain, and drew up a chair for himself.

The interview was scheduled to last no longer than ten minutes. But it was not until two hours later that Mary emerged from the drawing room with King Albert accompanying her to the car like any well-mannered gentleman.

During their time together, she had seen a young man worn with anxiety but still patient with her as she asked her questions. She had come, according to instructions, with no paper or writing tool and he had rummaged in the drawer of a plain pine desk until he found both. When she had pulled off her white kid gloves and put aside her muff and purse, everything had dropped to the floor. To her chagrin, he stooped and picked them up.

His answers were always fair even when he spoke of the atrocities. "Fearful things have been done, especially during the invasion, but it would be unfair to condemn the whole German army."

Mary asked about the invasion of the Germans into neutral Belgium. "Is it true the Germans protected their advance with Belgian civilians?"

"It is quite true. Again and again innocent civilians of both sexes were sacrificed to protect the invading army during attacks. A terrible slaughter."

They had talked on. Leaning an elbow on the mantel and smoking his pipe, King Albert expressed his admiration for America's President Wilson. He urged her to go to Louvain and Antwerp to see the destruction for herself.

"No one can tell you about it. You must see for yourself."

"I'm not certain I would be allowed to go, your Majesty."

He raised his hand as if brushing away a fly. "Nonsense. You are an American. You must see what happened: a country devastated, our wonderful monuments destroyed, our artistic treasures sacrificed without reason. Without justification."

"Not even as a necessity of war?"

"There is no justification for violation of neutrality, Madame," he said quietly but with a terrible strain in his voice.

Mary asked a few more questions and then knew she had already stayed too long.

Now they stood in the wind sweeping in from the sea, the King bareheaded, his pale hair blowing about. Mary sensed a terrible loneliness about this young man as he chatted with the general who was to return to Dunkirk with her, and she yearned to say something that might comfort him. But before she could gather the words, he turned toward her and reached out to shake her hand, smiled ever so slightly, and went inside.

The chauffeur helped her into the car. The Belgian general seated himself next to her and immediately began to exclaim in astonishment at the unprecedented length of her audience with the King.

But even as she responded, her gaze was directed to the young soldiers drilling along the hardpacked sand of the wide, level beach. There was no surf and the sea came in long flat lines of white. It was February and half of the Belgians who had rallied to defend their country against the German invasion last August were now dead. By the end of the week, she would return to England, but only for a week. When she came back, she planned to visit the French and British lines.

As the car careened around the potholes made by artillery shellfire, it struck her that here she was a lone American woman, thrust among some of the most exalted personages of the earth. And among some of the most humble. Divided between the timidity that comes from seeing indescribable horror and her ambitions, she suddenly felt much too small for the thing she had undertaken. Yet her pride pushed her to go on.

She had come to find out what was happening beyond the official barriers that guarded the Front so carefully. In the process, she had learned about the men who lived under these new and unspeakable conditions—what they thought and feared and hoped. She had taken notes and stored memories. She had a valuable story to tell.

When she finally returned to England from France, there would be more interviews: the Home Secretary, Winston Churchill and perhaps Queen Mary of England. By March, she would be home. Her original plan was to write about the Front, return to her family life, and go on to another story with no backward glances at what she had seen. After all, Americans believed the war in Europe was Europe's problem.

But something had happened to her. She had come to see, though unprepared to believe. A reporter, after all, was a skeptic by training. The kaleidoscope of experiences: the cheerful smiles of the Belgian soldiers, some no older than her young Stan and even fifteen-year-old Alan, as they marched past soaked by the icy rain; the silent endurance of the wounded;

the gentleness of the nurses and surgeons. The courage of a young king. All of it would haunt her.

She had come to realize that the brotherhood of man was a dream and that beneath Europe's shirt of diplomacy was a coat of mail. Every hour young men were sacrificed for political power. The enormity of the wasteful slaughter weighed on her like a leaden cloak. Surely, if this insanity were not stopped, the entire world was in jeopardy.

With an aching heart, Mary gazed out the window into the grey afternoon and knew that she had to make her countrymen understand. America must join the fight.

Chapter Thirteen

Mary ignored the frigid wind which numbed her face as she circled the deck of the steamship *Arabic*. In the two months in Europe, she had been her own person. Now that was about to come to an end. She had missed her family but not the responsibility of caring for them, and the realization bothered her.

Up to the last in London, she had been busy with interviews. She found Winston Churchill to be talkative but dull. Queen Mary of England was quite another matter. At the interview, the Queen was accompanied by a lady-in-waiting and wore a subdued green broadcloth suit, emerald earrings and a feathered hat. She was one of the loveliest and most charming women Mary had ever met.

The notebooks she had filled with her observations were in her trunk. Some entries had been scribbled as she sat in the back seat of a staff car as it tore along a rutted road, the lights out because it was near the Front.

The information though often nearly illegible was accurate, full of details of places, people, events. They were to serve as the basis of the articles for the *Post*. The first, her interview with the King of Belgium, was due for publication in only two weeks. Fortunately, she had already written the article but she still had to get the final approval of the Belgian government, which insisted on reviewing it to check on any breach of security.

She had set out to discover the truth about the war, and she was proud of her accomplishments. In the process, she had honed her reporting skills to a fine edge. Now she was eager to tell America what she had learned.

The day she walked in the door of her beloved house over-looking the Ohio, she took up family life once again. Ted and Alan hugged her and she exclaimed over how much they had grown. Stan stood behind her, laughing at everything and nothing. And then she realized that their son Stanley was missing.

"But, darling, you know he's up at school studying for the Harvard entrance exams," Stan reminded her.

She tried to smile. "Oh, of course. In all the excitement, I guess I forgot."

Her high spirits instantly vanished. It dawned on her that her family was no more impervious to change than the rest of the world. For months, she had held a mental image of the three boys together as they peered out of the silver frame at her. Now she realized it was just a picture. Their lives went on, with or without her.

Stan put an arm around her shoulders and led her into the study to a roaring fire and tea. The familiar silver tray set with bone china and the teapot she had found in Boston, the plate of dainty cucumber sandwiches were just as she might have ordered. She had no hand in their appearance, yet there they were. Somehow it made her feel unneeded.

By the end of the week, she was back in the familiar routine: breakfast, a talk with the cook about the day's menu, check with the housekeeper, and then to her study to write.

She was excited at the prospect of her meeting with George Lorimer, for she was anxious that he know exactly what she had planned for her articles.

But when she sat down in his office, he said, "America is

neutral, Mrs. Rinehart. Don't forget it. Give me a picture of London. Or Churchill. Or a sketch of General Foch at the Front. But no politics. Understand?"

"Men and women are dying over there, Mr. Lorimer. They're dying because Germany started a war it was fully prepared to wage and intends to win."

"I'm not convinced."

"It's not a French war or a British war or a Belgian war. It's a war about what this world is willing to accept as a standard of morality. Surely, you don't believe—"

Mr. Lorimer held up his long slender hand. "You know my position. God blessed us with the Atlantic Ocean to separate us from all that insanity. Besides, you know there's a matter of security. To reveal the name of every town and battery you visited and the location of every hospital would jeopardize the security of Allied battle plans."

She bridled. "I never intended to describe the specific places. It was the condition of the soldiers, their bravery, how much they need our help that I wanted to write about."

George Lorimer rose. "Let me repeat. Hearts and flowers, the woman's view, that's fine. But, Mrs. Rinehart, should you send me any balderdash about America joining the fight, I'll cut it. That I promise."

Mary knew it was pointless to argue and she caught the next train home.

In the morning, she sat down at her desk and began to write. The words told of what she had seen but not what she felt. The pages filled. She was doing what she had been paid to do but what she wrote were half truths and she felt like a hypocrite. Her neck ached. She could feel a tingling in her right arm. Her fingers began to cramp as if in protest against what she was forcing them to do. Only soaking them in hot water each evening relieved the pain.

She and Stan resumed their practice of inviting friends for dinner and the talk inevitably touched on her experiences.

Once she told of the horrible effect on the victims of the chlorine gas that the Germans used as a weapon.

"Darling, surely you're mistaken. We haven't heard a word about any of that," a close friend said.

"I tell you I saw men with their lungs seared," Mary insisted.

The men and women who sat at the table smiled at her as they might at an aging parent who had lost his faculties. Their smug faces infuriated her. She wanted to stand up and tell them to wake up. Don't you realize you're only told what the politicians want you to know, she longed to shout. Instead she changed the subject.

She seethed with anger. It was as if she was playing a toy whistle in a hurricane. Her frustration over the articles grew.

Yet the moment the April 3 issue of the *Post* that contained her interview with the King of Belgium hit the newsstands Mary became one of the country's celebrities. Her secretary was besieged with calls. Reporters wanted to interview her on every subject imaginable. Clubs pleaded with her to speak at their next meetings. She was flattered. But the questions from the audiences were inane, and when she offered insights on the war in Europe, the listeners' attention drifted away.

Chapter Fourteen

On May 7, the *Lusitania* was sunk by a German submarine off the coast of Ireland. Nearly two-thirds of the nineteen hundred passengers on board lost their lives. One hundred fourteen were Americans.

The next issue of the *Post* carried an article by former President Taft, favoring America's involvement in the war, and Mary's spirits rose. But only briefly, for as far as George Lorimer was concerned nothing had changed. The sinking of the *Lusitania* simply proved how war could drive any nation to brutality, he maintained in an editorial.

The bushes and fruit trees were brilliant with blossoms and the air pungent with their fragrance, but Mary hardly noticed. Whenever she drove past the mills along the river and heard the scream of the lathes as they turned out shells for Europe, her head was full of the remembered shriek as they flew over the desolation of No Man's Land. The country apparently was eager to profit from the war while it turned its back on the misery of dying men.

America was blind. Even the suffering at home was forgotten. What had happened to the cry for equal suffrage and child labor laws and the eight-hour day? It was as if the nation had stuck its collective head in the sand.

"I'm worried about you, darling," Stan said. "Just look at the circles under your eyes. Your color is bad. You might as well be fifty as thirty-nine."

Mary shrugged off his comments as if they were absurd but they hurt her deeply. Her mirror told her he was right. No amount of face powder helped. She was constantly tired and Stan suggested the family return to the French River for another summer of camping. But the idea held little appeal.

Then one day as she worked at her office in town, a tall, well-built man who looked to be in his late fifties walked through the door and introduced himself as Howard Eaton.

"Please excuse me, Mr. Eaton, but I'm afraid I don't—"

"We met at the Harrisons several years ago. I was back here on a visit."

"Of course." She put down her pen and smiled. Now that she looked at the man more carefully she recalled their meeting and learning that he was a Pittsburgh native who had gone west some years ago. He was a friend of former President Teddy Roosevelt, if she wasn't mistaken. "You have a ranch in Wyoming. Am I right?"

"You are indeed." He smiled and she noticed the brilliance of his blue eyes.

"In fact, I remember I was quite intrigued with some of your tales."

He laughed. "And every one of them true."

"Please, do sit down." Mary regarded him with amusement. The man had an easy manner, a directness about him, that she liked. He spoke well. Obviously a gentleman, he was well dressed despite the strange western style of his suit. She could not imagine why he had come to see her.

"Are you visiting family, Mr. Eaton?"

"I'm afraid distant cousins are all that remain of the Pittsburgh Eatons." He drew his chair a bit closer. "The fact is, I've come to ask a favor, Mrs. Rinehart."

"Oh?"

"You may be aware that the Glacier National Park opened in 1910. Well, it's fairly well developed now and we think the entire country ought to know about it. We want people to come out and see it. Which is where you come in."

She waited.

"I'm planning to take a party into the park on a kind of pack trip in July and I want you to come along."

"But why?"

"To write up the trip."

"Any newspaper man can do that. Why me?"

"You're a celebrity, Mrs. Rinehart. What you write, people will read."

She regarded him evenly. "Surely, you realize that I have obligations, Mr. Eaton. There are deadlines that must be met. And I have a family to consider." She smiled at him. "But thank you."

"Tell you what. Why not think about it for a while. Maybe over the weekend. I have some business in Washington but I plan to be back by Tuesday."

"I'm flattered. But I couldn't possibly. I'm sorry."

He rose, and with a genial grin, he said, "I'll come by next week."

Through the next two days, Mary could not push Howard Eaton's proposal out of her mind. The idea of striking off across the wilderness of Montana was luring: the vistas, the soaring peaks, the simple regime of living in the out-of-doors. But it was ridiculous and she decided not to even mention it to Stan.

Promptly at ten o'clock on Tuesday morning, the rancher from Wyoming walked through the door to her office and offered his hand.

"Good to see you again, Mrs. Rinehart."

"And you," she responded with a smile. It was as if they had been friends for years.

"I hope you have good news for me."

"Mr. Eaton—," she began. Chance encounters, lady luck, call it what one might, was an integral part of life. Never would she have imagined that Howard Eaton might step into her office with his outlandish idea. Yet he did. Now it was a question of whether to be sensible or whether to throw responsibilities to the wind and go.

As she looked at the man across the desk, she found herself instinctively gathering reasons to justify the trip. In the first place, she knew she could do an excellent job. The account would be a travelogue of sorts, for that's what Mr. Eaton expected but the keen eye she had nurtured in Europe would add a special dimension to it. Secondly, she desperately needed the change. Most of all, she wanted to go.

She smiled. "I've decided to go and see your park. Why don't you sit down and give me the details."

That night before dinner, she took the cocktail Stan handed her and broke her news.

"Why Montana? What's wrong with French River?"

"I've been there. This is some place new. All that dry air and sunshine will do me a world of good. And think of the marvelous material I'll get for stories." She put the long-stemmed glass down on the end table by her chair.

Stan eyed her, unconvinced. "You have never been on a horse more than two hours in your life and now you say you're going to make a three-hundred-mile trip in the wilds?"

She rose and kissed him. "That's exactly what I'm going to do, dear. And when I get back, I'll be a new woman."

But through dinner, she wasn't so sure. A trip, even this one, which would take her to faraway places, was merely an escape. It was not a cure.

Chapter Fifteen

Mary boarded the train on a muggy July day. Her bag was filled with what she hoped would be the appropriate clothing. Her gray riding suit with its long divided skirt and a long coat, Stan's old felt hat that she had worn all through France and Belgium, underwear, blouses, her high riding boots, and at the last moment she added her comfortable riding breeches. Tucked in the corners were her notebooks.

By the time she changed trains in Chicago and climbed on the Great Northern that would take her to Montana, she was beginning to see territory more foreign to her than the plains of Belgium. For the first time in months, she felt the weight of sadness and disappointment lift ever so slightly.

At dinner, she took a seat by the window. The steward stopped at her table and pulled out a chair. Behind him stood a well dressed couple. The woman, rather stout and about Mary's age, sat down and patted the seat next to her. Her husband took the seat across from Mary and smiled politely.

"Good evening," the woman said. "We're the McAllisters. Gladys and George McAllister."

"How do you do. I'm Mary Rinehart."

Mrs. McAllister's large brown eyes widened. "THE Mary Rinehart, the writer?"

"Well, I'm a writer."

"For heaven's sake." Mrs. McAllister lifted her napkin and dabbed it over her tiny mouth. "I don't suppose that you're going to Glacier National Park—with the Eaton party."

"As a matter of fact, I am."

"We are, too. And half the train, as far as that goes." Her mouth, which reminded Mary of cupid's bow, spread into a smile. "In fact, the young man in the seat across from ours is part of our group. Walter Wilson. From St. Louis. The family's in shipping, you know."

"Of course." Mary strained to smile. She had not the least interest in anyone's pedigree.

"And there's Miss Cramner," the woman added with an authoritative tone. "John Cramner's daughter. Chairman of the Board of Michigan Trust. Lovely girl."

The conversation dragged on and that night as Mary struggled out of her clothing in the lower berth, she realized how much the banal comments at dinner had tired her. Howard Eaton had told her that there would be about forty people in the group and she prayed they wouldn't all be like the McAllisters.

By morning, the train was rolling across treeless plains. Only an occasional house and barn and scattered clusters of boney range cattle interrupted the endless space. Trout was featured on the dinner menu. The dessert included some of the most delicious raspberries Mary had ever eaten. She stared out the window at the ragged line of mountains edging the horizon and marveled that they appeared no closer now than at midday.

At dawn, when she raised the shade to peer out at the passing scene, she discovered the plains were gone. In their place were U-shaped canyons. The mountains were closer now so that she could study their shape. But their size frightened her.

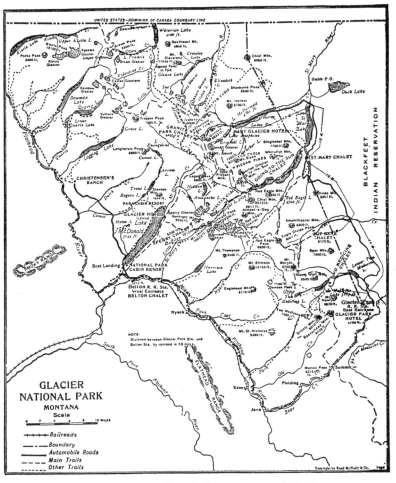

Glacier National Park, from a map of 1915.

At dusk, the train finally steamed to a halt in front of the Glacier Park station house.

Mary and the others climbed down stiffly into the cool air. Their luggage was unloaded and set on the cinders that lined the tracks. She looked around uneasily until she spotted Howard Eaton striding toward them. Behind him were half a dozen men in well-worn western garb, lounging against several battered trucks.

She stood at the edge of the milling group that gathered around Howard Eaton, noting how he shook each person's hand and looked him directly in the eyes as if he genuinely liked him. After a time, he saw her and made his way to her side.

"There you are, Mrs. Rinehart. Or may I call you 'Mary'? Glad you're here. We'll get the luggage to the hotel, have dinner, then everybody to bed. Need to get an early start tomorrow."

He offered his arm. "This way." And together, they walked toward several touring cars parked by the station house.

Mary's roommate turned out to be Florence Cramner. Tall and slender, she was slightly stooped as if by years of indecision. Her eyes were a washed out blue and she wore her blond hair in curls. Mary guessed she was about twenty-five. When they prepared for bed, she confessed that she had come along to recover from her father's recent death.

"I was an only child, you see. Mother died years ago. Father and I weren't close but he was all I had." Her eyes misted. "And I miss him."

Mary nodded in what she hoped was a sympathetic manner, and they climbed into bed and turned out the light. Something about people drawn together in strange places seemed to compel them to share confidences. It was a phenomenon she had noticed several times when she was in Europe. But she never grew used to it. She had no wish for Florence to say more and no intention of telling her anything. Bit by bit, she had managed to build the person she wanted the world to see. What lay beneath that façade was no one's business but her own.

Once dressed the next morning in her riding skirt and long coat, Mary packed her personal gear. She hoped she'd remembered everything. If not, it was too late now.

After breakfast, the party gathered and watched as the wranglers paired the riders and horses. Mary's mount was a buckskin named Gold Dollar.

"Sure-footed as a horse can get," the wrangler assured her as he tied Mary's duffle bag behind the saddle. The bundle was big and bulky so that it was almost impossible to swing her leg high enough to clear it without getting tangled up in her divided skirt when she climbed on.

Eventually, with all forty-two men and women mounted and their saddle cinches given a final check by the wranglers, Howard Eaton climbed on his magnificent white horse and gave the signal to start.

For a mile or so, the party moved in double file down the road from the hotel. Tourists watched and waved. A few followed in their automobiles. Mary sensed a feeling of excitement and high spirits among the group as if they were part of a parade. They passed a village of Indian tepees and a meadow scarlet with wildflowers. Finally, from the head of the line, Howard turned in his saddle and indicated with a wave of his hand that they were to turn off the road.

What was now a trail took a sudden plunge down the steep bank of a stream, its waters cascading over rocks and boulders. Mary rearranged her hold on the reins. The horses splashed across and moved on through the shadows of a narrow canyon. In a moment, they were out in open country again, heading toward the mountains they must cross.

Mary stared up at the towering peaks and tried to picture herself somewhere near their summits with the valley far, far below. A flick of fear passed through her. The trip was not going to be quite as easy as Howard Eaton had described it back in Pittsburgh.

Chapter Sixteen

Mary eased to the ground beside Florence and leaned toward the warmth of the campfire. The thick seams of the bulky riding skirt she had worn all day had rubbed saddle sores on her thighs, which made it almost impossible to sit comfortably in any position.

"If we could just leave these ridiculous skirts unbuttoned," she grumbled to Florence, slumped against a rock.

From across the campfire, the shrill voice of Gladys McAllister rose above the general hum of the group's conversation and Florence smiled. "But then there's Gladys to consider. Why, she'd go into shock if we did such a thing."

Mary laughed and then eyed her tentmate critically. "Florence, I think you ought to be in bed." The young woman, who never had been on a horse before, had ridden into camp so stiff and sore that she had to be lifted out of her saddle by a wrangler.

"I hate to go in so soon but I suppose you're right." Florence struggled to her feet. "But don't worry about disturbing me when you come in. I'll be sound asleep."

Mary watched to make certain the young woman made it safely back to their tent before she turned to survey her fellow travelers as they milled about the campfire. What a change a single day's ride made. Twelve hours ago, this group of arrogant socialites had larked about, joking, as if they were on a carousel ride; and tonight they sagged and complained.

Though Stan had finally agreed that the trip would be good for her, she was beginning to think it was the wrong time and with the wrong group. The sights and sounds of the war continued to haunt her, and she had nothing in common with these people and their petty grievances.

She felt a hand on her shoulder and glanced up to see Howard.

"How are you doing?" he asked with a smile.

"I'm all right."

He chuckled. "Then you're the *only* one in the party who is. I've already passed out enough liniment to sooth a small hospital full of sore muscles."

Mary tried to smile. "It's strange though. The others you invited on this trip seem so—" Mary began.

"Say, Howard, come here a minute, will you?" a man's voice called.

"Pardon me a moment, Mary. Seems I'm needed over there."

As Howard walked off, Mary pushed painfully to her feet and made her way slowly to the chuckwagon. It was probably just as well that her observations about the group had been interrupted, for what did it matter how she felt? She had come along on this trip of her own volition. She was here to do a job and she would do it.

At the moment, she didn't want to stay around the campfire, yet she didn't want to disturb Florence's privacy as she prepared for bed. Absently, she picked up one of the enameled coffee cups.

"More coffee, Miss?" asked the wrangler who served as the cook's helper.

"I suppose so. Thanks."

As she took a sip of the steaming liquid, she was suddenly aware of the sound of several men's voices. Their tone was intense and earnest. She glanced in the direction of the campfire and saw that it was Howard, Walt Wilson and Fred Condor who were engaged in the heated conversation. Intrigued, she moved closer.

"The government stole this land from the Blackfeet," Walt said.

Mary could see Howard, arms folded, his face set in a frown.

"Sorry, Wilson. You're way off base." Fred Condor was an engineer from Philadelphia whom she already had discovered held definite opinions on almost every subject. "The tribe has been paid. In fact, the government goes on paying. Every single month those Indians get their dole."

"You stand there and say the Indians get their payment? Not a chance. Not with those crooked agents they've got out here," Walt shot back.

"Hold on a minute, Walt," Howard cut in. "That's a pretty broad statement you're making. A few of the agents may not be honest but to lump them all together as a bunch of crooks is going too far. Besides, the railroads extended the tracks so the Blackfeet could get their beef to market."

Mary suddenly felt her reporter's instincts rise. She scented a story. In the months since she and George Lorimer had crossed swords, her interest in digging out truth had flagged. But there was something about this heated discussion which made her want to find out more. She moved closer.

"This is 1915. Are you saying there are still problems with the Indians out here?" she asked.

The men glanced at each other and for a moment said nothing. It was as if she had stepped across a line into territory where she was not wanted.

Finally, Fred said, "It's complicated, Mary. Certainly, it's not a subject a lady needs to worry about."

The condescending tone annoyed her.

"And, unfortunately, it's not a pleasant subject, Mrs. Rinehart," said Walt.

"Plus, it doesn't have a thing to do with your story of Glacier National Park," added Howard. "Now if you'll excuse me, I've got to get everyone packed off to bed. We start early in the morning."

The other two men and Mary stood in awkward silence as Howard walked away.

"Well, gentlemen, it seems we have our orders," she said, trying to control her anger. "The wagonmaster has spoken. So I wish you a good night."

The men nodded and stepped aside. The light of the campfire was dim so she couldn't be sure, but as she passed Walt, she thought she saw a glimmer of amusement in his eyes.

Once inside the tent, Mary pulled in a deep breath and tried to calm down. Florence groaned softly in her sleep. As quietly as possible, Mary undressed and slid into her bedroll. The thought of Howard presuming to tell her what was or wasn't the story of Glacier National Park infuriated her. The man was as high-handed and manipulating as any general who had tried to block her stories in Europe. Howard could run the pack trip, but he wasn't going to run her.

Chapter Seventeen

ime to get up! Everybody up!"

Mary awoke, stiff and sore, as Howard's voice echoed through the camp, and she crawled painfully from her bedroll. How could she even get on a horse, much less ride all day?

Her riding skirt lay folded at the foot of the bedroll. She eyed it for a moment, already determined that never would she wear that cumbersome thing again. Dragging her bag from the corner of the tent, she reached into its depths and pulled out her well-worn riding breeches. No more saddle sores for her. These were what she'd wear, no matter what the narrow-minded western conventions decreed.

With the hated riding skirt stuffed safely in the bag, she continued dressing. Leaving Florence to sleep, she stepped outside. The aroma of strong coffee wafted through the cool air and she walked toward the cook tent. A group was already seated at the long eating table and as she approached, she heard someone gasp.

"Good heavens," Glady's voice rang out. "Just look what Mrs. Rinehart's wearing."

Mary straightened her shoulders and continued toward the breakfast table. Walt Wilson, standing by the chuck wagon, grinned at her and she grinned back. His ruddy complexion and muscular build reminded her more of a wrangler than a young man who spent his days inside an office.

On the oilcloth-covered table were round tins of butter, jars of molasses, and platters piled high with bacon, ham, fried eggs, and flapjacks. Tin plates, enameled cups, spoons and forks had been placed at one end.

Mary sat down and reached for the welcome cup of coffee set at her place.

"Well, that's quite an unusual get-up you're wearing this morning," came Howard's voice behind her.

She looked around and smiled brightly. "Oh? Eastern women have worn riding breeches for years."

The woman across the table raised an eyebrow and Mary gave her a level look. I couldn't care less what you think of me, she wanted to say to her. Today I'm going to be comfortable and you're not. And she proceeded to eat her breakfast.

When it was time to mount, Mary pulled up into the saddle with no trouble at all. The other women in their riding skirts struggled as she had yesterday to lift their legs and arrange the skirts over their saddles and packs.

As Florence was hoisted into her saddle, Mary flinched in sympathy at how painful the operation must be. After breakfast, she had gone back to the tent to try to talk her out of riding today. But Florence remained adamant and Mary admired her courage.

The long line of riders started out with Howard in the lead and Walt right behind him. With the two together, it might be an excellent chance to pursue her questions about the Blackfeet. But she decided now was not the time.

They moved along at a leisurely pace. On either side were meadows of scarlet paintbrush and beyond, stands of aspen and pine. After a while, Howard signaled the group to veer off onto what appeared to be an old animal trail, and the climb began.

Mary had never liked heights, and almost immediately her stomach began to feel queasy. The trail steepened, twisted, and

"The idea of striking out across the wilderness of Montana was luring: the vistas, the soaring peaks, the simple regime of living in the out-of-doors."

turned as it continued upward. Howard had said the trip would be over mountain terrain, but he had not mentioned that the trail would be only a few feet wide, nor that it would cling to the side of a mountain.

She glanced out of the corner of her eye at the edge of the trail. Beyond was nothing but sky. The queasiness grew. Being stuck on a horse, on a narrow trail, the edge of which dropped at least half a mile straight down, was almost worse than being at the war front. But if she was frightened, she could only imagine how terrified Florence was.

With teeth clenched, Mary told herself over and over not to look down. She closed her eyes and prayed they'd soon be at the top.

At last they reached a tree-covered area Howard called "the bench." It was relatively wide and flat, and the group paused to enjoy the view. As Mary breathed a sigh of relief, she reached over to pat Gold Dollar's neck, thankful that instead of picking her way along the outer edge of the trail, the mare had hugged the cliff wall.

No more than a few minutes later they headed upward again. Mary desperately tried to control her growing nausea. She drew a deep breath, and then another until gradually she became aware of the fresh, crisp air. Immediately, she began to feel a little better.

When they finally reached the summit, she chanced a glance downward and spotted the trees on the bench where they had stopped to rest. Now they looked no larger than twigs. Off toward the horizon were snowy peaks. As she gazed out in all directions, she felt a rush of exhilaration. She could see for miles. It was if she was on the rooftop of the world.

They began to start down. Mary leaned back in her saddle, more relaxed, and her thoughts of the Blackfeet returned. From the heated conversation around the campfire last night, it appeared that there was a real question about how well the government was carrying out its responsibilities to the Indians. Were there unscrupulous Indian agents in charge? It peaked her curiosity. She wanted to find out the facts.

They climbed another pass, taking switchback after switchback. Thankful for Gold Dollar's steady ways, Mary began to get used to the heights.

The beauty spread out before her made her forget her fear. Where else but in the high mountains could she see such scenery?

"Well?" Howard's voice jogged her thoughts. "What do you think?"

"It's—breathtaking. There's no way a person could appreciate how beautiful it is without seeing it. I'm eager to write about it, Howard. Once people know about Glacier Park, how could they possibly resist coming to see it?"

"I told you you'd like it."

The trail was wider now, and for a while they rode companionably side by side. Howard pointed out Baring Creek running through the scooped-out valley below and Citadel Mountain in the distance with Blackfeet Glacier cradled against its side.

They rode on in silence for a few minutes. It was the first time she had been alone with him all day and she decided to bring up the matter of the Blackfeet.

Choosing her words carefully, she said, "Howard, you know I'm a reporter."

He glanced over at her and grinned. "That's why you're here."

She smiled into his blue eyes which had a way of disarming a person. "You remember last night and the talk about the Blackfeet Indians? I think there's a story there. And I intend to get it."

He shrugged. "Mary, the Indian problem has been around for sixty years. You can't hope to find out the whole story on a trip like this."

She had agreed to write the story of Glacier National Park. And Howard had made it plain the Indians had no part in it. But her reporter's instincts told her he was wrong. The question boiled down to how she could find the facts to prove it.

Chapter Eighteen

W hen they finally reached camp, Mary watched as Florence was helped off her horse and how cautiously she made her way toward their tent. Dinner was already set out on the planks that served as the eating table, so Mary picked up two plates of food and took them with her to the tent.

"I thought you might like to eat in here." Mary handed a plate to Florence.

With a grateful smile, the young woman took the plate of beefsteak and fried potatoes. "Don't you want to be out there with the others?"

Mary coughed a laugh and shook her head. "Ever since I came out wearing my riding breeches, those 'ladies' have avoided me as if I had the plague and the men have treated me like a 'fallen woman'."

"But you're Mary Roberts Rinehart. You're famous. You can wear whatever you want to."

"I know. And I intend to keep doing just that." She eased down to sit on her bedroll and inspected her plate. "Smells good, doesn't it?" And she began to eat.

"Mrs. Rinehart, I"—

Mary stopped cutting her meat and looked up to see that Florence's eyes were full of tears.

"When I got off my horse yesterday, I thought my legs would collapse. I was ready to give up and go home." She wiped her eyes with her sleeve. "Then today I tried again and I really didn't know if I'd make it or not. But, Mrs. Rinehart, I did make it. I rode the whole distance."

"You did indeed, and you should be proud as punch." Mary smiled. "Now. I don't want to see a single morsel of food left on that plate. You have a long ride ahead of you tomorrow."

After she returned the plates to the cook tent, Mary went in search of Howard, Walt, and Fred Condor. If Florence could get back on her horse in spite of her pain, she could confront these men and get her Indian story. Not to her surprise, she found them, with coffee cups in hand, standing by the campfire again.

"You know perfectly well that all of the land around here—including Glacier Park—used to be the hunting grounds of the Blackfeet," Walt was saying. "Admit it. They were cheated out of almost four-fifths of their land."

Howard shook his head. "I'll admit there are problems. But the Indians weren't cheated. Besides, what about the white settlers? They have their side, too."

Mary moved closer. "What do you mean?"

Fred gave Mary a cool glance.

"Westward expansion was inevitable," Howard said. "I'm a good example. I came west to ranch. I needed grazing land for my cattle. Believe me, I sympathize with ranchers." He reached down and tossed a small stick into the fire. "Still, it's only right that the Blackfeet should be treated fairly."

"And they aren't?" Mary asked.

"I guess I'd have to say that's a matter of opinion," said Howard. "The real problem is that they're victims of change."

"Victims is right," said Walt.

"You sound like all the other do-gooders, Wilson," said Fred. "But say. If we're going to continue this discussion about the Noble Savage, let's find a place to sit. I'm tired."

Mary moved with the three men to a vacant spot near the fire. Once settled, she pulled out her notebook and pencil from the pocket of her jacket.

"Now," she said, "when did this problem begin?"

"The problem, as you call it, started about sixty years ago," said Howard. "But maybe I'm getting ahead of myself. How much do you know about the Blackfeet?"

"Well, nothing really," Mary replied.

"The Blackfeet in Montana are related to tribes in Canada—the Siksika, or Blackfoot proper, the Blood and the Northern Piegan. Actually, the Blackfeet in Montana are Southern Piegan."

Mary shifted her weight and tried to find a more comfortable spot. Though less stiff than last night, she still felt the effects of two days' long rides.

"The Blackfeet traditionally were hunters," Howard continued. "They depended on the buffalo for everything—food, clothing, lodges. They used every part of the animal."

"And then the people from the East began to move out here," interrupted Walt. "They wanted ranches, roads, telegraph lines, so they simply took over the Blackfeet hunting grounds."

"Good Lord, the Blackfeet didn't own the land," said Fred, angrily.

"You're right," said Howard.

"Maybe so. But the Blackfeet's existence depended on buffalo," countered Walt. "They hunted this whole area—hundreds of miles in all directions. And then the whites started coming in. They invaded this land. Overran the hunting grounds, the sacred burial grounds, everything. They slaughtered the buffalo. And just for the sheer sport of it."

Eyeing Walt with the look of a patient father, Howard lit his pipe. "Well, anyway, sixty years ago—back in 1855—the government drew up a treaty. The Lame Bull Treaty. And the Blackfeet agreed to it."

Mary jotted down the names and dates.

"The treaty gave U.S. citizens the right to come into Blackfeet land in return for $20,000 a year 'in useful goods and services' for ten years and $15,000 a year for ten years for 'civilizing the tribe'," Howard added.

"Sounds reasonable," said Fred. "Pretty generous terms, if you ask me."

Walt shot him an angry glance. "The 'useful goods' turned out to be rice and moldy bread—neither of which the Blackfeet liked."

"And what did 'civilize the tribe' mean?" Mary asked.

"It meant the government planned to make the tribe into farmers because the imbeciles in Washington thought farming was more 'civilized' than hunting," growled Walt.

"Oh, come on, Wilson," said Fred. "That's about enough of your propaganda."

Walt sat up. It was obvious to Mary that there was more to this Indian question than treaties and money. If the strong emotions of these three men were any indication, the subject affected people deeply. And she sensed she was hearing only a small part of a complex matter. Her body ached but she couldn't leave. She looked from one man to the other. Who was right?

"Gentlemen, all these facts are fascinating," she said. "But I'm no closer to understanding the Blackfeet problems than I was in the beginning. If you wouldn't mind, let me ask about the treaty. Exactly what—"

Howard stood up. "Sorry, Mary. We'll have to continue your education later. Right now, it's show time."

And with the sound of bells, seven Indians suddenly stepped out of the shadows and into the firelight.

Chapter Nineteen

As Mary watched Howard make his way across the campsite toward the Indians, her anger rose. How dare he speak so condescendingly about "continuing her education." And why, when he knew she wanted to write about the Blackfeet, hadn't he told her they were coming to the camp?

Howard led the Indians over to the campfire and Mary leaned forward to get a better view of them. One man was dressed in a buckskin shirt and trousers and moccasins. Long fringe cascaded from his shirt sleeves and the outside seams of his trousers. His gray hair was plaited in two braids and on his head was a large feathered headdress.

The other men were bare to the waist and bare-legged. Squares of buckskin hung from strings around their waists, covering buttocks and private parts. Each square was decorated with feathers set in a circular pattern, and in the middle of each circle was a small round mirror. The moccasins and necklaces and headbands they wore were beaded. Attached to the back of each man's headband was a single feather.

A sudden hush fell over the circle of campers. People stared wide-eyed at the Indians. All but Fred, who sat leaning back on his elbows, obviously amused.

"Well, what do we have here?" he said. "Looks like the shades of Buffalo Bill and his Wild West Show." He laughed.

Howard placed a hand on the shoulder of the Indian dressed in buckskin.

"Chief Three Bears brought some of his braves to entertain us tonight. They're going to perform some of their tribal dances. So let's give them a welcome," he said and began to clap. For an instant, the campers glanced at one another uncertainly and then joined in.

Howard returned to the circle and sat down beside Mary. On the other side of her, Walt muttered under his breath.

"For once old Fred's right. This IS just a show. You're not going to see any real tribal dances here."

Mary eyed Walt, noting the hard set of his jaws.

"What do you mean?"

"It's all for tourists," said Walt. "Louis Hill—the fellow who owns the Great Northern Railway—brings the Blackfeet in from the reservation to entertain his customers. Good publicity for his railroad and hotels. That's all it is."

Meanwhile, the Indians had arranged themselves in a circle around the campfire. Three Bears sat on the ground with a large drum in front of him, and as he tapped the drum, the men began to dance. The dancers moved with intricate steps to the steady beat of the drum, chanting as they danced, from time to time punctuating their chants with a shout.

Mary watched in fascination as the dancers turned and twisted, bent low to the ground and then straightened, moving round and round in the circle. Bells jingled, mirrors flashed. Even the flames of the campfire seemed to be part of the dance.

The campers stared as if they were hypnotized until the dance ended. As the applause died down, Mary turned to Howard. "I want to talk to those men."

Howard gave her a look of amusement. "You're welcome to try, but you won't get far."

Mary rose and dusted off her breeches. "I'll manage."

The Indians were busy gathering up the drum and blankets

they had brought. As she came closer to them, she paused and glanced back to see that Howard, Walt and Fred had followed her.

"Say, Three Bears," called Howard. "Before you and your braves leave, here's a lady who'd like to meet you."

Three Bear's back was straight as a bowstring. But standing beside him now, Mary saw that he was a very old man. His hands were gnarled, his face was etched by a mass of wrinkles, and his mouth was puckered from lack of teeth.

"This lady's a warrior woman," said Howard. "She's just come back from a battlefront."

Three Bears eyed Mary, glanced down at her riding breeches, and smiled.

"Warrior woman," he repeated. He turned to the other Indians and spoke words Mary couldn't understand. The men nodded.

"Three Bears here is ninety-three years old," said Howard. "But he can still ride a horse better than some men half his age."

The old man smiled slightly, deepening the creases around his eyes and mouth.

"Mrs. Rinehart's a very important person. She writes stories, and she has many friends in Washington where the Blackfeet's 'Great Father' lives."

Three Bears regarded Mary solemnly for what seemed like several minutes. "Ah, yes. A very important person."

Again he turned to his braves and translated, but this time the men responded and the seven engaged in a discussion of some kind. After a few minutes, he turned back to Mary.

"We will make warrior woman a member of the Blackfeet." He nodded to Howard. "We will come back tomorrow."

And abruptly he turned away, signaling the men to follow.

Mary stared after them for a moment, stunned yet intrigued by what she thought she had just heard. "Blackfeet don't really initiate white people into their tribe, do they?"

"Sure," Howard said.

"You mean it happens all the time?"

"No. But it does happen."

Walt gave a hard laugh. "It happens when Louis Hill decides to put them up to it." His eyes narrowed. "Hill thinks the Blackfeet are 'his' Indians. He brings them in, gives them a good meal, then sends them out to impress the tourists."

"Now wait a minute, Walt." The muscles below Howard's jaw tightened. "You have no cause to say that. The Blackfeet take these ceremonies seriously. They don't initiate just anybody."

"Oh, come on, Howard," said Walt. "You can't pretend these dances and initiations aren't Hill's publicity stunts."

Fred laughed. "This man Hill sounds like a regular P.T. Barnum."

His smile suddenly faded. "But seriously, Howard, you're not going to hold up our pack trip for a day just to kowtow to those Indians, are you?"

Mary looked from one man to the other. Perhaps Walt was right about the initiation's being just a show. Or perhaps Three Bears and the other men might think that if she was a member of the tribe, she would take up their cause. Whatever was the case, membership in the tribe could provide her with an entree to the Blackfeet and the story she was determined to get.

"Would an initiation really hold up the party as much as Mr. Condor says it would, Howard?" Mary gave Fred a sideways glance. "We wouldn't want to spoil the trip for him . . . or, of course, for anyone else."

"Actually, we'll have to spend an extra day here anyway," said Howard. "The supply truck hasn't gotten in, and we can't go on until it does."

On her way to her tent, Mary began to plan her strategy for interviewing members of the tribe.

"Mrs. Rinehart," someone called, and she turned to see Walt striding after her. "I just wanted to say something."

Mary waited for him to catch up with her.

"I've heard about these initiations," Walt said. "Even though I'm convinced they're publicity gimmicks, I haven't ever heard that the Blackfeet initiated a woman into the tribe before."

"Well, then, this will be something different. I'm sure my three sons will be impressed."

The next morning the Indians arrived dressed in buckskin shirts and trousers. Strips of red flannel had been woven into their long braids. Three Bears and another man whom he introduced as Chief Tail-Feathers-Coming-Over-the-Hill, wore large feathered headdresses.

Howard had told her that the park photographer would be on hand, and Mary briefly considered digging out her riding skirt for the occasion. But she decided against it, and wore her usual riding breeches, cotton blouse, hip-length coat, and Stan's old hat.

Before the ceremony began, the Indians formed a semicircle around Tail-Feathers. Three Bears announced the name of each man. Now in the daylight, Mary saw that most of them were young, probably in their twenties. Chief Tail-Feathers, a small man nearly a head shorter than Mary, could be about forty.

Stab-By-Mistake, a heavy set man, was the drummer. He sat on the ground near the semi-circle, darting glances at the crowd of campers. He and his friends nodded and spoke to one another in low tones. Occasionally, they smiled at each other as if enjoying some private joke.

The park photographer set his camera on its tripod near the Indians. Gladys and several other women clustered near the cook tent; Walt stood with Florence and Fred in the shade of a tall pine; Howard circulated among the campers.

Three Bears motioned Mary to a place in front of the Indians, and Stab-By-Mistake started to tap his drum. Chief Tail-Feathers waved a long-fringed ceremonial pipe to the four directions, the ground and the sky.

"He is making an offering to earth, sun, and the four winds," explained Three Bears.

The chief puffed the pipe and handed it to Eagle Child beside him. Each man in turn smoked and handed the pipe on. When the pipe had made its rounds, three men walked to a large bundle tied with leather thongs.

Two-Guns-White-Calf, with a black felt hat like Stan's, pulled out a beaded paint pouch and placed it at Mary's feet. Black Bull, who wore pants made from a Hudson Bay blanket, brought her a beaded dagger sheath. Yellow Wolf, tall and good looking, unfolded a large, black buffalo hide before her. Every man's face held a solemn expression.

Mary glanced around. Walt stood apart with his arms crossed over his chest. Gladys was still by the cook tent with her gaggle of followers, and Florence had joined Howard. Fred was nowhere in sight.

The drum started again and the men began to chant. Suddenly, the sounds stopped. Tail-Feathers looked at Mary and announced in a loud, clear voice, "Your name is Pitamakin."

"Pitamakin was a Blackfeet warrior woman," said Three Bears. "In English, the name is 'Running Eagle'."

Pitamakin, Blackfeet, the towering peaks beyond—they belonged to another world and yet at this instant they seemed far more real than the war or her family.

"Pitamakin? Warrior woman?" Three Bears' voice startled her.

"Yes, Three Bears. Thank you for the honor you have bestowed upon me. I want to thank the others, too."

She stepped forward.

"Thank you, Chief Tail-Feathers. I am honored." She smiled and bowed her head.

"Yes." The man's eyes looked through her as if she was a pane of glass.

As she stepped from one man to the next, each met her glance with a cold stare. She was confused and puzzled. It was as if they were angry about her initiation into their tribe.

She turned to Three Bears again. "Three Bears, I want to find out more about the Blackfeet. I want to talk to your people."

"Pitamakin, the warrior woman who has friends in Washington, will help our people." His face was unsmiling.

"Help? In what way?"

[148]

"Our people starve. The supplies don't come. The 'Great Father' in Washington does not keep his promise to the Blackfeet."

Mary felt a surge of energy. This was her story. But she couldn't take Three Bears' word. She had to find out for herself. She'd have to find Indians who could talk to her. She'd have to see their problems first hand.

"I must come to your village, Three Bears."

He nodded.

"I promise I'll do what I can."

As the campers gathered at the long table for dinner that night, Mary sought out Howard, for she was anxious to learn his side of Three Bears' story that the Blackfeet were starving.

"Something's wrong out here, Howard. I don't really understand it, but I intend to find out what's going on."

Out of the corner of her eye, Mary saw Gladys take a seat next to Walt.

"And how does it feel to be an Indian, Mrs. Rinehart?" she cooed, giving Walt a sidelong glance as if to check his reaction to her remark.

For an instant, Mary was tempted to say something unpleasant or ignore her completely. But when she caught the small grin at the edge of Walt's mouth, she smiled at her sweetly and said, "That's interesting you ask, Gladys. Actually, it doesn't feel a bit different than it feels to be a white woman." And she turned back to Howard.

"Three Bears says the Blackfeet are starving, that their supplies don't arrive."

"Maybe the Indians don't get as much food as they think they should have," Howard admitted. "But I know for a fact that the agent sends rations."

"Howard, I want to go to the reservation. I want to see the situation for myself."

"Old Three Bears really got under your skin, didn't he?"

She bridled. "To say that his tribe is starving is serious. I can't let that go by, Howard."

"Look, Mary, you don't know anything about Indians. They

[149]

don't trust whites, and they won't talk to you. You'd be wasting your time."

"Three Bears talked to me."

"True. But he's the only one who would. And half of what he says you can't believe."

Mary felt her annoyance growing and she busied herself with eating. Howard obviously was not going to help her get the information she wanted. And he could be right that the Indians wouldn't talk to her, for this morning she had felt a wall between herself and the Blackfeet. Even Three Bears showed no real friendliness.

She stabbed at the slice of ham on her plate, no longer hungry. Here was a story right in front of her nose. Yet she couldn't catch hold of it. Just as she thought Howard didn't object to her idea, he pulled back, telling her that the Indians couldn't understand English or even those who could wouldn't speak to her. And then there was the attitude of the Indians themselves. Three Bears had seemed to almost demand that she come to the aid of the Blackfeet at the same time the other men greeted her with stony stares.

Once or twice in Belgium and France she had almost given up hope of getting the story she was after. She had battled Lorimer over what she could write. But never had any story been so elusive as this one about the Blackfeet.

Chapter Twenty

Mary walked slowly along the creek bank out of sight of the camp. The long shadows cast by the tall pines seemed as dark as her mood. A log lying near the bank extended into the water out toward a large boulder in the middle of the creek.

She stepped across it and seated herself on the boulder. The water tumbled past. Now and then a fine spray sifted over her face and clothes. Reaching down into the icy stream, she opened and closed her fist. To get the Blackfeet story was as impossible as grasping a handful of water.

It seemed as if she had lost her touch. And the more she thought about the deadlock she was in, the more dispirited she became. The shadows were stretching into night and the air grew cooler. Soon it would be dark and she got to her feet and stepped back across the log to the bank.

When she returned to camp Howard, Walt, and Fred were helping the wranglers unload the supply truck that had finally arrived. Watching them, the idea of what she must do suddenly seemed clear. She approached Howard.

"I've decided to ride back to Glacier Lodge with your supply truck. Tomorrow I'll hire a car at Glacier and drive out to the Blackfeet Reservation."

Howard set down the crate he had just pulled from the truck.

"Mary, I can't let you wander off by yourself. You're a member of this party. I have a responsibility for you. You have to stay with the group. That's all there is to it."

"You're wrong, Howard. I go and do what I please."

"Oh, for heaven's sake, Mary, be sensible. No woman—not even you—can go traipsing off alone to an Indian reservation."

Mary eyed him for a moment and then turned to Walt.

"How about you, Walt? Will you go with me?"

A wide grin spread over his face. "I'd be honored."

Howard slapped his hat against his thigh. "Just hold on a minute, you two. How in the world do you think you're going to find any Indian camps?"

Mary smiled. "Why, I thought I'd get Three Bears to guide us. We have to pass the Lodge on the way out to the reservation, and you know he's usually around there somewhere."

The old Indian agreed to Mary's plan, and the next day all three started for the Blackfeet Reservation with Walt at the wheel of the hired car, Three Bears in the back seat, and Mary, notebook and pen in her lap, next to Walt.

"You told me yesterday that your people are starving," she said to the chief.

"Last winter was the worst for many years. The agent told us to drive our cattle to the east part of our land. But rustlers stole our herd."

"And who's to say that agent wasn't in cahoots with the rustlers?" asked Walt.

"We had nothing left. No cattle to send to market in Chicago. No meat for our people to eat," said Three Bears.

"My grandfather had a ranch out here for a while in the early '80s," interjected Walt. "He used to tell about when the ranchers saw all that good grazing land on the Reservation, they just went ahead and let their cattle feed on it illegally. One year there were a quarter of a million head on Indian land."

Mary jotted down the figures.

"The winter of 1883 six hundred Blackfeet starved to death. The buffalo were gone. The ranchers' cattle had driven out the other wild game." Walt hit the steering wheel with the heel of his hand. "And to top it all, the crooked Indian agent made off with the tribe's rations."

"Here," put in Three Bears. "This way." He pointed left to a meadow of tall grass.

Walt turned off the road to follow rutted wagon tracks leading through fields of dried grass.

"The other evening, Walt, you said something about Louis Hill and the railroad. What's that all about?" Mary asked.

"James Jerome Hill—Louis' father—wanted to push his Great Northern Railway into Blackfeet territory."

"So?" Mary adjusted the notebook in her lap.

"Well, the ranchers and the railroad teamed up. They got some politicians on the payroll and before long the Blackfeet found themselves signing the Sweet Grass Treaty."

Mary looked up from her notebook. "Tell me about it."

"Well, the Blackfeet agreed to sell their rights to four-fifths of their land for three million dollars. But the government whittled them down to half that amount."

Mary tapped her pen against her notebook. "Didn't anyone in Congress stand up for the Indians?"

"Not a soul," said Walt.

The more she learned about the government's treatment of the Indians, the less she liked it. At last, she spied what looked like a cluster of white dots off in the distance.

"Look, Three Bears, over there," she said.

"That is the camp," he said.

As they drove closer, the dots became tepees and about fifty yards from the camp, Three Bears told Walt to stop.

"Make a sound with the horn," he said. "To let them know they have visitors."

As they waited, the sound of dogs barking drifted through the open car window. Before long, two Indians appeared and started walking toward the car. The men, dressed in buckskins, greeted Three Bears in words Mary couldn't understand.

"They want us to follow," explained Three Bears.

Mary quickly gathered up her pencil and notebook from the car seat. At last, she was to get her story.

The camp consisted of twelve canvas tepees. Thin trails of smoke rose from the center of each tepee. Wooden farm wagons were parked beside several of the tepees. Beyond the camp, a small herd of horses grazed in the open meadow.

As Mary approached the camp, several other Indians appeared from inside their tepees. A woman, old and hunched, leaned on the arm of a younger woman with two little children peeking from behind her skirts.

A strange hush began to settle over the camp. As she passed the tepees, the women stood outside them like silent sentinels. There were no sounds—no children's laughter, no dogs barking. With Three Bears at her side, Mary walked on until two men, both very old, emerged from their tepees.

"Three Bears, please explain that I am Pitamakin, the warrior woman," said Mary. "Please tell them I've heard they are starving. Tell them I want to help them."

"Some of the men can speak to you in English," Three Bears said. "They will speak to you."

An old man stepped forward. "Last winter was very bad. There was no food. Children died." Tears filled his eyes.

"The agent did not send help," said a young man.

"No help from the 'Great Father' in Washington," added another old man.

Mary eyed the old man. Although he spoke to her directly, she realized that he didn't see her. To be blind at his age was not unusual. But she had a nagging suspicion that the blindness was a sign of something more serious.

"I would like to see all the people of the camp," she said.

A young man stepped forward and introduced himself as Gray Duck. "I will show you."

As he moved from one tepee to another, he called in a low voice and several women and children appeared.

"Where are the other men of the camp?" Mary asked.

Gray Duck's eyes narrowed. "They work on the government irrigation project."

"And are they paid for that?"

"The government pays a little for work. But then it does not send rations. The Blackfeet are hunters, not farmers. We do not know how to farm," said Gray Duck. "We do not want the irrigation project. Yet the government forces our people to work on it."

Mary shook her head. "The government seems to think it knows what's best for you."

She walked slowly around the camp and looked carefully at each person's eyes. Some were swollen and inflamed and crusted with yellow mucous. From her nurse's training, Mary recognized the signs of trachoma. If a person rubbed his eyes or touched another, the disease would spread. Without treatment, the inflicted people would go blind.

"Where is the Reservation hospital?" she asked Three Bears.

"There is no hospital."

"But what about a doctor?"

"No doctor."

"But when your people are sick . . . when the children are dying . . . where do they go?"

"Doctors are far away. They do what they can."

Mary felt her anger rise. These people were suffering, yet no one in Washington paid attention. She thought of her years at the Homeopathic Hospital and of the pitiful human beings she had cared for. These Indians needed help as much as any of those people, yet they didn't have even so much as a student nurse to ease their pain. Mary no longer cared about getting a story. She just wanted to help these people.

"Three Bears, does anyone in this camp know how to read and write?"

"Gray Duck went to a white man's school."

"Gray Duck, I want you to write to me," said Mary. "Tell me what is going on here at the Reservation. I live many miles away, but I won't forget your people. Somehow, I'll find a way to help you."

Mary walked slowly back to the car. She'd lost faith in America when it had turned its back on Belgium and France. But her country's treatment of the Blackfeet was equally as shameful. The Blackfeet were Americans. And the country had turned its back on them.

Chapter Twenty-one

Mary leaned back against the stiff leather seat of the car and covered her eyes with her hand. The way out to the Reservation had seemed long but the return trip was endless.

Her head throbbed with thoughts of the terrible discovery she had made. She had wanted to get a story, to put a feather in her cap after George Lorimer refused to print the facts about the war. But instead of a story, she had uncovered a raw wound on America's soul.

No one spoke as they retraced their route through the meadow, over the wagon track, and up the main road to Glacier Park. When at last they reached Glacier Lodge, Mary was exhausted. With her last bit of energy, she paid for the use of the car, made arrangements for a horse for the next day, and climbed the stairs to her room to fall into bed.

The next morning, Mary and Walt set out on horseback to join Howard and his party. In place of her sure-footed little mare Gold Dollar, Mary now rode a mount named Moll. The route they had to travel was steep, the trail was narrow.

It wasn't until they were well on their way that Mary discovered Moll was not a riding horse but a pack animal. The mare was trained to stay away from the cliff wall where one bump of the pack load might throw her off balance. Instead she picked her way along the outer edge of the trail.

As they climbed the mountain, Mary's left leg dangled over the abyss, and the terror she'd felt on her first days on the trail returned. "Don't look down," she said to herself over and over again. She counted every step Moll took. But how many steps would there be until they were over the pass?

"Don't move in the saddle. Just sit still," she repeated, silently.

Suddenly, Moll dislodged a rock and Mary's heart stopped. Her stomach turned a somersault. The rock bumped down into the valley below, down, down, until the sound disappeared in space.

At last, they reached the summit. She took a deep breath and as they started down, her mind again focused on the problems of the Blackfeet. In a few days, she would be on her way home to Pittsburgh. And then to Washington to find the help the Blackfeet must have. She would see the Commissioner of Indian Affairs and extract a commitment from him that the Indians would receive the food and the medical care they so desperately needed.

The elevator door closed behind her and Mary again checked the directions on the slip of paper in her hand. "Basement, Justice Department Annex, third office on the right."

She tucked the note back in her handbag and stared down the long, dimly lit hallway. At the third door, she paused, her hand on the oval brass doorknob. The sign on the frosted glass panel read, "Homer Webb, Commissioner of Indian Affairs." She went in.

The receptionist was seated at a cluttered desk in front of a closed door. No light showed beneath it.

"May I help you?" The woman peered over the top of her reading glasses. She was thin and wore her gray hair in a bun at the back of her neck.

"I'm Mrs. Rinehart. I have an appointment with Commissioner Webb."

"I'm sorry, but he's not in. He was called out of town yesterday. He'll be away for at least a week."

"But I have an appointment. I came all the way from Pittsburgh just to speak with him."

The woman sighed. "I'm very sorry. I did try to reach everyone who had appointments." She glanced sadly at an appointment book. "Could I schedule you for another time perhaps?"

Mary silently counted to ten as she tried to control her temper. "No, I have to return home this weekend. Is there someone else I might speak with?"

"Well, you could talk to a member of the Senate Indian Committee, I suppose."

Mary brightened. "Would you have a list of the committee?"

The woman frowned. "I'm sure there's a list around here somewhere." She walked to a file cabinet, pulled open a drawer and began to rummage through it.

"It must seem we're not very well organized but there's always so much to do." She pulled open a second drawer.

Mary flicked open her pendant watch and checked the time. She had already wasted nearly half an hour.

"Miss, please don't bother about the list. Perhaps you might remember a few of the names of the senators on the committee."

"Oh, yes. Senator Hazelton Ainsworth is one. You could probably find him in his office in the Senate Office Building."

Senator Ainsworth's office was on the second floor half way down the long front hallway. Mary stepped inside and introduced herself to the pretty young receptionist and explained the purpose of the visit.

"Are you one of the Senator's constituents?" she asked sweetly with a soft southern accent.

Mary smiled. "No, but I'm very much concerned about the welfare of the Indians, and I understand the senator is a member of the Indian Committee."

The girl glanced at an appointment book. "Well, I'm afraid he can't see you today. But if you'd care to come back next week"—

"Is Senator Ainsworth in his office now?"

The girl looked startled. "Well, yes, but he . . . he's busy."

"Will you please tell him that Mary Roberts Rinehart would like to discuss an important issue with him."

"Well, ah"—

Mary drew off one glove, then the other. "I'll wait."

Senator Ainsworth came forward to meet Mary as she entered his office. He was tall and paunchy, with narrow, close-set eyes and a thick thatch of iron-grey hair that made his head look huge.

"Mrs. Rinehart, come in. Please sit down." He indicated the chair opposite his desk.

"Thank you, Senator."

"My wife will be interested when I tell her I've met you. She reads your stories from time to time."

"Oh, does she?" Mary smiled.

The senator leaned back in his high-backed chair and folded his hands across his stomach.

"And, now, what brings you to Washington?"

"I've just returned from a trip to Montana. While there, I visited the Blackfeet Reservation. Senator Ainsworth, I can't tell you how appalling the conditions are among those Indians."

"I'm sure you realize, Mrs. Rinehart, that the Indian problem is extremely complicated. It has many facets one must consider."

"Those people are starving, Senator."

"My dear lady, they receive shipments of supplies regularly."

"That's not what I was told. And, I might add, my information came from a variety of sources."

Ainsworth's eyes narrowed. "A person such as yourself who hasn't studied the situation can't possibly understand."

"I've been there. I've seen that they're starving." She looked him straight in the eye. "I've also seen that many are going blind with a disease called trachoma; and I've seen that there is no hospital, nor even a doctor on the Reservation."

Ainsworth sighed deeply. He sat up and leaned his elbows on the desk.

"Mrs. Rinehart, you're well-meaning. You're upset. You want to do good things for the Indians. For which I commend you. But you don't understand the many facets of a complex situation."

Mary clutched her handbag and took a deep breath.

"Senator Ainsworth, the Indians of Montana might be called wards of the United States. We've taken their land, pushed them onto a reservation, and now we must take care of them."

"I can assure you the government tries to do just that. What you don't understand—and it's a sad commentary on the situation—is that the Indians steal from each other."

"What do you mean 'steal from each other'?"

"Why, my dear lady, it happens all the time." He gave her a tight smile. "The government sends rations, the amounts carefully calculated, for all children, elderly and infirm. But what do the Indians do?"

His eyes narrowed. "They share the rations with their able-bodied relatives. And as a result the supplies are gone long before the next rations arrive."

"Senator Ainsworth, a facet—as you call it—which you and others like you don't understand is that Indian societies are communal. What belongs to one, belongs to all."

She drew on her gloves. "But I can see I'm wasting my time here." She stood up. "I'll go somewhere else to find help for my Indians."

Back at the hotel, Mary made a list of people who might be able to get her an appointment with the Secretary of the Interior. The third telephone call brought results. Her friend called back to say that Secretary Franklin Lane would see her the next morning at eleven o'clock.

She lifted her freshly pressed Paris suit from its hanger and slipped into it. In becoming shades of rust and brown, it had the fashionable hemline just grazing the ankle. She lifted her new hat from its box and adjusted it on her head. Made of the same brown velvet to match the trim on her suit, it had a puff crown and narrow brim. She smiled in satisfaction at her reflection in the full-length mirror.

The receptionist ushered Mary into Franklin Lane's office at precisely eleven. The room had a high ceiling, mahogany-paneled walls, and a gleaming wood floor covered with richly hued Oriental rugs. Tall windows looked out on a view of tree tops with the Washington Monument in the background. Thomas Eakins paintings were arranged on the walls.

"Mrs. Rinehart, please come in."

The secretary, of medium height and build, offered his hand as he came toward her.

"Here, please sit down." Lane ushered her to an armchair and returned to his place behind the desk. "Now, what may I do for you?"

"Mr. Secretary, I've just returned from Montana where I visited the Blackfeet Reservation. I found that the Indians don't have enough to eat, and they don't have proper medical care. The conditions are deplorable."

Lane raised an eyebrow as if surprised.

"But they receive monthly food supplies, Mrs. Rinehart, and there is a doctor who visits the tribe regularly."

"I visited one of their camps. I talked with the people. I'm a trained nurse, Mr. Secretary, and I saw with my own eyes that many of them are suffering from trachoma. Something must be done to help those people."

"I can understand your concern. But surely the camp you saw was an isolated case."

Mary pulled five letters from her handbag and laid them on the desk.

"These letters, Mr. Secretary, are from Blackfeet living in various camps on the Reservation."

Lane picked up the letters, glancing quickly at each one.

"The actual writing was done by one of the younger men, but the elders dictated what they wanted to say."

He returned to the first letter and studied it.

"You'll notice that they signed with red thumbprints. I think the red means 'blood,' Mr. Secretary. Those Indians are telling you that they are dying."

Lane put down the letters.

"I'm wondering, Mrs. Rinehart, if perhaps these letters might paint conditions as worse than they really are."

He handed them back to her.

"You see, we receive regular reports from our superintendents," he said. "The reports state when, and how much, food and supplies are delivered."

"I met one of your superintendents, or 'agents' as most people out there call them. Your department had fired that agent from his job—and good riddance."

Mary eyed Lane. "And I have the feeling that there are others out there who are just as unscrupulous as he was."

"That's a big statement, Mrs. Rinehart."

"Starvation and disease are big problems, Mr. Secretary."

"Indeed they are. However, I'm sure that the appropriate people have matters well in hand."

Putting the letters back in her handbag, she rose.

"Thank you for seeing me. I'll take no more of your time." She snapped her handbag shut. "However, I promise you, Mr. Secretary, I'll not rest until something is done to help those Indians."

As she rode the elevator down to the main floor, Mary silently fumed. Lane seemed unwilling to admit any wrongdoing in his department or even to investigate the possibility. Her time in Washington was almost gone and she had run out of ideas of who else she could see that might help her.

Mary hailed a cab and set off for the hotel. As she glanced out the window, she decided that perhaps she should treat herself to a shopping spree and a leisurely lunch at a fashionable restaurant. Perhaps then her mind would be clear enough to think of something else.

When she finally returned to the hotel and let herself into her room, the telephone was ringing.

A woman's voice said, "Mrs. Rinehart? Secretary Lane is on the line. Hold on please."

Mary sat down on the bed.

"Mrs. Rinehart, since you left my office I've thought about what you said. As a result, I've directed my assistants to check into the Blackfeet situation. And I want you to know I'll do all in my power to do what's necessary."

Mary drew a deep breath. "That's good news, Mr. Secretary. I can't tell you how much I appreciate your help. I'll continue to be in touch with you."

Mary returned to Pittsburgh, satisfied that at last the Blackfeet would receive the help they needed. Her persistence in Washington had paid off. Now she could turn her attention to other pressing matters—writing, family, social obligations.

But her satisfaction was short lived. Two months later she received a letter from Gray Duck.

"Our people still have no doctor. The agent tells us he will not send rations. He says we are paid to work. How can we work on the irrigation project in the big snows?"

Mary stared at the letter in her hand. She felt numb. After his words of assurance, Franklin Lane had done nothing. The Blackfeet would starve, go blind, perhaps freeze to death—and there was nothing she could do.

Chapter Twenty-two

That winter the Blackfeet were never out of Mary's mind. She had nightmares about children with shrunken bodies, old men with glassy stares, women too weak to tend their babies.

"Darling, this Indian business is consuming you," Stan told her. "You're going to end up in the hospital the way you're pushing yourself."

Mary shrugged off his concerns but when she sat down at her desk to write, her thoughts returned to the suffering, here in this country and overseas—that dark cloud on the horizon.

Work was piled high. She had the Glacier book to finish for Howard, a new mystery novel to complete, and articles to write for *The Saturday Evening Post.* She kept forcing herself to get the work done.

Depressed, angry, feeling ill, she wrote letters to Secretary Lane. His replies were long but said nothing. She wrote letters to Gray Duck and his answers confirmed her fears that the Indians continued to suffer. Finally, she decided the only way to get any action on the problem was to go again to Washington.

This time Lane was less cordial. Seated at his desk, he glanced up from the papers spread in front of him. "Yes, Mrs.

Rinehart." His voice was cool. "Please sit down." He motioned to the chair across from him.

Mary seated herself and began to draw off her gloves.

Opening a large tan folder, Lane pulled out a sheaf of papers. "I've been looking over the correspondence we've received from you over the past few months."

He shuffled through the letters. "Your concern for the Blackfeet is admirable. When you were here last fall, I told you I'd look into the situation. I've done that."

Mary waited.

"In these letters you continually refer to sending supplies and medical assistance. But you seemingly fail to understand the allotment system."

"On the contrary, Mr. Secretary." Mary regarded him evenly. "The allotment system carves up the Blackfeet land, giving every man a small slice and telling him to go out and grow crops on it. Because he's supposed to earn his way, you cut off his rations."

Lane took a deep breath, and tapped his fingers on the desk. "The system has been studied and found to be workable."

"You're mistaken, Mr. Secretary. The Blackfeet are hunters, not farmers. They don't know how to grow crops."

"Mrs. Rinehart, we've sent people out there to TEACH them how to grow crops."

Mary ignored the interruption. "But what is worse about the allotment system is that it breaks up their culture. The Indians have traditionally owned everything in common—land, cattle. And when they hunted, the whole tribe shared the food."

She leaned forward, eyeing him directly. "Unfortunately, Mr. Secretary, you and the Congress fail to recognize these facts."

"We're fully aware of the Blackfeet culture." His voice rose a decibel. "But, in practicality, their system no longer works. It doesn't encourage independence, which is what the Congress wants for them."

"Do you think starvation and blindness encourage independence?" Mary rose to leave. "I can see that my visits and letters have been useless." She drew on her gloves. "Perhaps

"These Indians needed help . . . yet they didn't even have so much as a student nurse to ease their pain. Mary no longer cared about getting a story. She just wanted to help these people."

newspaper and magazine articles, exposing this indifference to the real needs of the Indians, would have more effect." With a tight smile, she added, "Of course, I hope I'll not have to resort to that."

Mary returned to Pittsburgh more dejected than ever. The months went by, and she continued to push herself. She met deadlines, gave speeches, entertained friends, and kept the family organized. She continued to send letters to Lane. She felt weighed down by work and by worry about the Blackfeet and about the war.

Only when the boys were home and the family was together did her spirits rise. On one such afternoon late in the spring, young Stanley and Alan lay sprawled on the grass in the shade of an elm as Ted wrestled with Floss the collie and Mary and Stan lounged in lawn chairs.

"Say, everyone, how would you all like to go on a trip with me this summer to visit the Blackfeet Indians?" she asked.

Ted tried to push Floss away. "I would, I would! When can we leave?"

"Do you really mean that, Mother?" Alan sat up.

"Of course, I mean it. Gray Duck says they're having a conclave of chiefs at the Reservation. They want me to come."

Young Stanley laughed. "First a member of the tribe, and now hobnobbing with the chiefs. What's next for the 'warrior woman'? Are they going to make you a chief, too, Mother?"

"Be serious, Stanley. It's important for me to go. I need to see for myself if conditions have improved." She glanced at Stan. "I don't learn a thing from Lane's letters. All he ever does is repeat government policy."

Mary decided they should leave for Montana the first week in July. She wrote Lane of her plan, and assured him that if conditions on the Reservation had not improved, she would follow through on her promise to write articles about the situation. She also asked him to send a note that she could give the Blackfeet at the conclave. She tried to be persuasive.

. . . You are the 'Great Father' of the Blackfeet, not the President, and they will feel that for once in their lives they are in touch with you.

Lane answered with a long letter, explaining recent legislation for the Indians. But he sent no note. Mary wrote back.

But, dear Mr. Secretary, where is my friendly little message for my Indians?

One morning, a week before the family was due to leave for Montana, Mary sat at the breakfast table, sipping coffee. Across from her was Stan, partially hidden by the newspaper. She picked up the morning mail which the maid had placed in front of her and began to glance through it. Suddenly, a letter from the Department of the Interior caught her eye. She slit it open and began to read.

Tell the Indians that you and I are friends and that we shall do all that we can for them as one friend would do for another.

"Secretary Lane! That idiot! No wonder the Indians are starving and dying. Just look at this ridiculous letter."

Stan peered around the newspaper.

"Here, look at this." She held out the letter to him.

He put down the newspaper and reached for the sheet.

"Have you ever read anything so inane?"

Stan frowned. "It doesn't say much, does it?" He handed the letter back.

"No more than any of his other letters have." She slapped the letter down on the table, ignoring the coffee that sloshed from her cup. "Not one person in Washington really cares about the Indians."

"Darling, you're shouting."

"We have the Homer Webbs who are not in their offices

when they're supposed to be—we have the Hazelton Ainsworths who are intolerable—"

"Mary, please—the servants. They'll hear you."

"And the crowning blow is that we have a Secretary of the Interior who will not even write a nice little note to my Indians." She pushed herself up from the table, knocking her chair backwards. "Believe me, Stan, if I find that the Blackfeet still don't have their rations and medical help, I'll write an article about Lane and his department that will set Washington on fire!"

Mary sent another, more strongly-worded, letter to Lane, and for the next week she watched the mail for his reply. No letter came. The day of the family's departure arrived, and still no word.

She was in a turmoil. How could she face the Blackfeet chiefs when she'd failed them so miserably? She'd failed her boys, too, for she had assured them of a warm welcome from the Indians. But there'd be no chance of that now.

The train ride to Montana seemed endless. She wished she'd called the whole trip off. With every click of the wheels, her tension increased. When they finally pulled into Glacier Park station, a headache, which had been no more than a twinge at the base of her skull when they left Pittsburgh, had grown into a throbbing mass of pain.

As she stepped onto the station platform, a wave of nausea swept over her. She glanced quickly from one end of the platform to the other. There were no Blackfeet in sight.

"Where are the Indians, Mother?" Ted asked. "You said they'd be here to meet us."

"I don't know." She could only force a whisper.

"Look," Alan said. "Down there. Someone's waving."

At the far end of the platform, beyond a group of tourists, a man in a gray suit started toward them. It was Howard Eaton.

As he neared, Mary saw that he was holding up a book.

"They tell me I've got the first copy off the press." He grinned down at Mary. "See those words: *Through Glacier Park*, by Mary Roberts Rinehart."

Mary took the book and leafed through it. "So you have a copy even before the author." She smiled. The sight of the new book made her feel a trifle better.

"You did a great job on it, Mary," said Howard. "And Louis Hill agrees with me."

"I'm glad you and Mr. Hill like it. But, Howard, where are the Indians? Gray Duck said he and the others would meet us."

"They're not coming. Gray Duck asked me to meet you," he said.

Mary's knees felt ready to buckle. "But, I must see them— talk with them."

"Yes, Mr. Eaton, we've been looking forward to meeting Mother's Indians," Young Stanley's eyes twinkled.

"Good. Let's get going then."

On the ride out in Howard's touring car, Mary sat in silence while Stan and the boys plied Howard with questions about the park. She wished she'd never suggested that Stan and the boys come. If Gray Duck and the chiefs had refused to meet them at the station, they would hardly give the Rineharts a friendly reception at the Reservation.

The route Howard took was unfamiliar to Mary for unlike her first visit they did not leave the main road. After they had driven for some miles, she saw what looked like a building in the distance. When they were about thirty yards away, Howard stopped the car.

The building was constructed of logs. About twenty feet long and ten feet wide, it had a door in front and a small window on each side of the door.

Mary and the boys followed Howard up to the building. He knocked and the door opened.

Gray Duck stood in the doorway. "Welcome, Mrs. Rinehart. We've been waiting for you and your family. Please come in."

Mary, puzzled as to what was going on, stepped across the threshold. Howard, Stan and the boys followed. It took a few minutes for her to adjust her eyes to the dim light that filtered through the windows. At last, she could make out seven Indians standing behind Gray Duck.

"These chiefs and I want to honor you and your family, Mrs. Rinehart," said Gray Duck.

Mary sucked in her breath.

"Look around you." Gray Duck pointed to stacks of boxes around the walls. "The supplies you promised arrived last week. In addition, the agent tells us that from now on we will have a nurse on the Reservation, and a doctor will visit us once a month."

Mary's pulse raced. She had succeeded in making Secretary Lane and the Interior Department pay attention to her Indians. She hugged the Glacier book to her breast. Looking around the room at her Blackfeet friends, she knew in her heart that there was hope for this country that she loved. America would not forever turn its back on the suffering of other peoples, nor on the suffering of its own.

AFTERWORD

Mary Roberts Rinehart was deeply troubled by the United States's lack of support for Britain, France, and Belgium in the early months of World War I. After returning from her Glacier trip the summer of 1915, she wrote an article for *The Saturday Evening Post* entitled "The Altar of Freedom." In the article, which subsequently was published in book form, she urged American mothers to send their sons to war.

She pointed out that because she was a woman, she could not serve in the military, but she was "doing a far harder thing. I am giving a son to the service of his country." Three members of her family—Stan, Stanley Jr., and Alan—enlisted.

Yet Mary was burdened by a sense of guilt, knowing that many young men would be killed or maimed. In her autobiography she wrote, "I finished (the "Altar of Freedom") in agony of spirit . . . after twelve hours of unbroken effort. I had cried until I was exhausted, but at last it was done. . . . Perhaps only God knows what a terrible thing that was to do, or how it haunts me now."

Her work in behalf of the Blackfeet Indians, however, brought her a large measure of satisfaction. She confronted Secretary of the Interior Franklin Lane, "armed with notes

. . . and with the memories of those tragic old full-bloods, clasping my hand and then telling their pitiful tales." And she succeeded in bringing about some changes in the system. "From that time on I became a sort of mother-confessor, adviser and friend to the tribe."

NOTES

Chapter Nine

Excerpts from Mary Roberts Rinehart small maroon notebook, memorabilia of World War I and war diary I, Rinehart collection, Hillman Library, University of Pittsburgh.

Chapter Ten

Excerpts from Mary Roberts Rinehart war diary I and II, Rinehart collection, Hillman Library, University of Pittsburgh.

Chapter Twelve

Excerpts from Mary Roberts Rinehart war diary II, Rinehart collection, Hillman Library, University of Pittsburgh.

Chapter Twenty-two

Excerpts from correspondence, Indian Office, Blackfeet General, U.S. Department of Interior, File No. 5, 1, Part I, Office of the Secretary, June 15, 1908–August 9, 1929.

BIBLIOGRAPHY

Rinehart, Mary Roberts, unpublished autobiographical fragment, approximately one hundred holograph sheets, some fifty of these typed and edited, written about 1954, Rinehart collection, Hillman Library, University of Pittsburgh.

Rinehart, Mary Roberts, war diary I, II (January 8–February 4, 1915), small maroon notebook, Rinehart Collection, Hillman Library, University of Pittsburgh.

Correspondence regarding the Commission on Conservation and Administration of Public Domain (1929–1933).

Correspondence, Indian Office, Blackfeet General, United States Department of the Interior, File No. 5, 1, Part I, Office of the Secretary, June 15, 1908–August 9, 1929.

Cohn, Jan, *Improbable Fiction, The Life of Mary Roberts Rinehart.* Pittsburgh: University of Pittsburgh Press, 1980.

"Homeopathic Hospital and Dispensary of Pittsburgh," *History of Allegheny County, Pennsylvania,* Vol. I, Chicago: A. Warner & Co. Publishers, 1889.

Bibliography

Maloney, Sue, ed. *Glen Osborne Reflections 1883–1983.* Sewickley Historical Society, Sewickley, Pennsylvania, 1983.

Rinehart, Mary Roberts. *Through Glacier Park.* Boston: Houghton Mifflin, 1916.

———. *My Story.* New York: Farrar and Rinehart, 1931.

———. *"K".* Boston: Houghton Mifflin, 1915.

———. *Kings, Queens and Pawns.* New York: Doran, 1915.

———. *Nomad's Land.* New York: Doran, 1926.

———. *The Doctor.* New York: Farrar and Rinehart, 1936.

———. *Tenting Tonight.* Boston: Houghton Mifflin, 1918.

———. *The Altar of Freedom.* Boston: Houghton Mifflin, 1917.

———. *The Amazing Interlude.* New York: Doran, 1918.

———. *The Breaking Point.* New York: Doran, 1921.

———. *The Out Trail.* New York: Doran, 1922.

———. "Woman on a Dude Ranch." *Harper's Bazaar,* April 9, 1932.

———. "The Family Pays the Bill." *Ladies' Home Journal,* March, 1935.

———. "The Man Upstairs." *The Saturday Evening Post,* June 18, 1949.

———. "Your America and Mine." *Cosmopolitan,* July 1932.

Tuchman, Barbara W. *The Guns of August.* New York: Macmillan Publishing Co., 1962.